THEBES OF THE HUNDRED GATES

ROBERT SILVERBERG

Thebes of
The Hundred Gates

HarperCollins*Publishers*

HarperCollins*Publishers*,
77–85 Fulham Palace Road,
Hammersmith, London W6 8JB

Published by HarperCollins*Publishers* 1993

9 8 7 6 5 4 3 2 1

First published by
Pulphouse Press 1992

A catalogue record for this book is
available from the British Library

ISBN 0 00 223975 2

Set in Garamond ITC

Printed in Great Britain by
HarperCollinsManufacturing Glasgow

For Joe and Gay Haldeman –
– many a cup of kindness yet –

Heaven is opened, the company of gods shines forth!
Amon-Re, Lord of Karnak, is exalted upon the great sea!
The Great Nine are exalted upon their seats!
Thy beauties are thine, O Amon-Re, Lord of Karnak!
— *The Liturgy of Amon*

O Flame which came forth backwards, I have not stolen
the god's offerings.
O Bone-breaker who came forth from Heracleopolis, I
have not told lies.
O Eater of entrails who came forth from the House of
Thirty, I have not committed perjury.
O You of the darkness who came forth from the darkness,
I have not been quarrelsome.
O Nefertum who came forth from Memphis, I have done
no wrong, I have seen no evil.
— *The Negative Confession*

CHAPTER ONE

The sensory impact pressed in on him from all sides at once in the first dazzling moment of his arrival: a fierce bombardment of smells, sights, sounds, everything alien, everything much too intense, animated by a strange inner life. Luminous visions assailed him. He wandered for some indeterminate span of astounded time in shimmering dream-forests. Even the air had texture, contradictory and confusing, a softness and a roughness, a heaviness and a giddy lightness. Egypt coursed through him like an uncheckable river, sparking and fizzing, stunning him with its immensity, with its stupefying aliveness.

He was inhaling magic, and he was choking on it. Breathing was a struggle – he was so stunned that he had to remind himself how it was done – but the real problem was the disorientation. There was too much information and he was having trouble processing. It was like sticking not just your fingertip but your whole head into the light-socket. He was a dozen different sizes and he was experiencing every moment of his life, including moments he hadn't yet lived, in a single simultaneous flash.

He had prepared for this moment for months – for nearly all his life, you might almost say – and yet nothing could really prepare anyone for *this*, not really. He had made three training jumps, two hundred years, then four hundred, then six hundred, and he thought he knew what to expect, that sickening sense of breathlessness, of dizziness, of having crashed into the side of a mountain at full tilt; but everyone had warned him that even the impact of a six-C jump was nothing at all compared with the zap of a really big one, and everyone had been right. This one was thirty-five C's, and it was a killer. *Just hold on and try to catch your breath*, that's what the old hands had told him, Charlie Farhad who had made the Babylon jump and Nick Efthimiou who had seen the dancers leaping over bulls at the court of King Minos and Amiel Gordon who had attended a royal bar mitzvah at the temple of Solomon when the paint was still fresh. *It's a parachute jump without the parachute*, Efthimiou had said. *The trick is to roll with the punch and not try to offer any resistance. If you live through the first five minutes you'll be okay.* You built up a charge of temporal potential as you went, and the farther back in time you went, the stiffer the charge, in more ways than one.

Gradually the world stopped spinning wildly around him. Gradually the dizziness ebbed.

The actual extent of what he could see was quite limited. They did their best to drop you off someplace where your arrival wouldn't be noticed. He was in an unpaved alleyway maybe six feet wide, flanked by high walls of dirty whitewashed mud-brick that blocked his view to either side. The last bright traces of the golden aura of the jump field were still visible as a series of concentric rings with him at its center, a glittering spiderweb of light, but they were dwindling fast. Two donkeys stood just in front of him, chewing on straw, studying him with

no great curiosity. A dozen yards or so behind him was some
sort of rubbleheap, filling the alley almost completely. His
sandal-clad left foot was inches from a row of warm green
turds that one of the donkeys must have laid down not very
long before. To his right flowed a thin runnel of brownish water
so foul that it seemed to him he could make out the movements
of giant microorganisms in it, huge amoebas and paramecia,
grim predatory rotifers swimming angrily against the tide. Of
the city that lay beyond the nasty, scruffy little slot where he had
materialized, nothing was visible except a single tall, skinny
palm tree, rising like an arrow against the blank blue sky above
the alley wall. He could have been anywhere in any of a hundred
Asian or African or Latin American countries. But when he
glanced a second time at the wall to his left he caught sight of a
scrawled graffito, a scribbled line of faded words hastily
applied; and the script was the vaguely Arabic-looking squig-
gles and dots and boxes of Eighteenth Dynasty hieratic and his
well-trained mind instantly provided a translation: *May the
serpent Amakhu devourer of spirits swallow the soul of Ipuky
the winemerchant, may he fall into the Lake of Fire, may he be
trapped in the Room of Monsters, may he die for a million
years, may his ka perish eternally, may his tomb be full of
scorpions, for he is a cheat and a teller of falsehoods.* In that
moment the totality of the world which he had just entered, the
inescapable bizarre reality of it, came sweeping in on him in
tidal surges of sensation, Thoth and Amon, Isis and Osiris,
temples and tombs, obelisks and pyramids, hawkfaced gods,
black earth, beetles that talked, snakes with legs, baboon-gods,
vulture-gods, winking sphinxes, incense fumes drifting upward,
the smell of sweet beer, sacks of barley and beans, half-
mummified bodies lying in tubs of natron, birds with the
heads of women, women with the heads of birds, processions

of masked priests moving through forests of fat-bellied stone columns, water-wheels turning slowly at the river's edge, oxen and jackals, cattle and dogs, alabaster vessels and breastplates of gold, plump Pharaoh on his throne sweating beneath the weight of his two-toned crown, and above all else the sun, the sun, the sun, the inescapable implacable sun, reaching down with insinuating fingers to caress everything that lived or did not live in this land of the living and the dead. The whole of it was coming through to him in one great shot. His head was expanding like a balloon. He was drowning in data.

He wanted to cry. He was so dazed, so weakened by the impact of his leap through time, so overwhelmed. There was so much he needed to defend himself against, and he had so few resources with which to do it. He was frightened. He was eight years old again, suddenly promoted to a higher grade in school because of his quick mind and his restless spirit, and abruptly confronted with the mysteries of subjects that for once were too difficult for him instead of too easy – long division, geography – and a classroom full of unfamiliar new class-mates, older than he was, dumber, bigger, hostile.

His cheeks blazed with the shame of it. Failure wasn't a permissible mode.

Maybe it was time to start moving out of this alleyway, he decided. The worst of the somatics seemed to be past, now, pulse more or less normal, vision unblurred – *if you live through the first five minutes you'll be okay* – and he felt steady enough on his feet. Warily he made his way around the two donkeys. There was barely enough clearance between the beasts and the wall. One of the donkeys rubbed his shoulder with its bristly nose. He was bare to the waist, wearing a white linen kilt, sandals of red leather, a woven skullcap to protect his head. He didn't for a moment think he looked convincingly

Egyptian, but he didn't have to; here in the great age of the New Empire the place was full of foreigners – Hittites, Cretans, Assyrians, Babylonians, maybe even a Chinaman or two or some sleek little Dravidian voyager from far-off India – *tell them you're a Hebrew*, Amiel had advised, *tell them you're Moses' great-grandfather and they'd better not fuck around with you or you'll hit them with the twelve plagues a hundred years ahead of schedule.* All he had to do was find some short-term way of fitting in, keep himself fed somehow until he had completed his mission, sign on for work of any sort where he could simulate a skill – a scribe, a butler, a maker of pots, a fashioner of bricks. Anything. He only had to cope for thirty days.

The alley took a sharp bend twenty feet beyond the donkeys. He paused there for a long careful look, fixing the details in his mind: the graffito, the rubbleheap, the angle of the bend, the height and declination of the palm tree. He was going to have to find his way back here, of course, on the thirtieth day. They would be trawling through time for him, and that was like fishing with a bent pin: he had to give them all the help he could. For a moment his heart sank. Probably there were fifty thousand alleys just like this one in Thebes. But he was supposed to be an intelligent life-form, he reminded himself. He'd make note of the landmarks; he'd file away all the specifics. His life depended on it.

Now at last he was at the end of the alley.

He peered out into the street and had his first glimpse of Thebes of the Hundred Gates.

The city hit him in the face with a blast of sensation so heavy that he felt almost as shaken as he had in the first instant of the time-jump. Everything was noise, bustle, heat, dust. The smell of dung and rotting fruit was so ripe he had to fight to keep from gagging. There were people everywhere, huge throngs of them, moving with startling purposefulness, jostling past him, bumping him, pushing him aside as though he were invisible to them as he stood slackjawed in the midst of all this frenzy; this could be New York's Fifth Avenue on a spring afternoon, except that many of them were naked or nearly so in the astonishing furnace-like heat, and huge herds of goats and sheep and oxen and asses and weird long-horned hump-backed cattle were moving serenely among them. Pigs snorted and snuffled at his feet. He had emerged into a sort of plaza, with tangled clusters of little mud-walled shops and taverns and, very likely, brothels, all around him. The river was on his right just a few dozen steps away, very low but flowing fast, a swift green monster cluttered with hundreds of ships with curving prows and towering masts, and right in front of him, no more than a hundred yards distant, was a vast walled structure which, from the double row of giant papyrus-bud stone columns and the hint of intricate antechambers beyond, he supposed was the building that in modern times was known as Luxor Temple. At least it was in the proper north-south alignment along the Nile. But what he saw now was very different from the temple he had explored just two weeks ago – Two weeks? Thirty-five hundred years! – on his orientation trip to contemporary Egypt. The Avenue of the Sphinxes was missing, and so were the obelisks and the colossi that stood before the great flaring wings of the north pylon. The pylon didn't seem to be there either. Of course. The Luxor Temple sphinxes were Thirtieth Dynasty work, still a dozen centuries in the future. The obelisks and colossi were the doing of Rameses II, whose reign lay five or six kingships from now, and so too was the north pylon itself. In their place was an unfamiliar covered colonnade that looked almost dainty by Egyptian architectural standards, and two small square shrines of pink granite, with a low, slender pylon of a clearly archaic style behind them, bedecked with bright fluttering pennants. He felt a small scholarly thrill at the sight of them: these were Twelfth Dynasty structures, perhaps, ancient even in this era, which Rameses' inexorable builders had no doubt swept away to make room for their own more grandiose contributions. But what was more bewildering than the differences in floor plan was the contrast between this temple and the bare, brown, skeletal ruin that he had seen in latter-day Luxor. The white limestone blocks of the façades and columns were almost unbearably brilliant under the sun's unblinking gaze. And they were covered everywhere by gaudy reliefs painted in mercilessly bright colors, red, yellow, blue, green. From every cornice and joist glittered inlays of precious metal: silver, gold, rare alloys. The temple pulsed with reflected sunlight. It was like a second sun itself, radiating shattering jolts of energy into the frantic plaza.

Too much, he thought, beginning to sway. Too much. He was overloading. His head throbbed. His stomach lurched. He was having trouble focusing his eyes. He felt chills even in the midst of all this heat. Because of it, most likely. He imagined that he was turning green with nausea.

'You are ill? Yes, I can see that you are ill, very ill.' A sudden deep voice, virile and harsh. A hand closing tight around his wrist. A man's face thrust practically up against his, thin lips, hawk nose, shaven scalp. Dark brooding eyes bright with concern. 'You look very bad. You will be an Osiris soon, I think.'

'I – I –'

'To die like a pig in the street – that is not good, not good at all, my friend.'

It was astonishing that anyone had spoken to him, and even

more astonishing – despite all his training – that he could understand. Of course they had filled his brain with Egypt, pumped him to the brim, language, art, history, customs, everything. And he had learned a good deal on his own before that. But still he was surprised to find that he had comprehended the other man's words so easily. His tutors hadn't guessed quite right on the pronunciation, but they had been close enough. The vowels were wrong, everything shifted into the back of the throat, 'e' turning into 'i', 'o' turning into 'u,' but he was able quickly enough to adjust for that. His benefactor was holding him upright with that vise-like grip; otherwise he would fall. He tried to think of something to say, but no words would come. His fluency failed him when it was his moment to speak. He couldn't frame a single sentence. *You will be an Osiris soon.* Was he dying, then? How strange, putting it that way. He must be starting to look like Osiris already, the dead god, green-faced, mummified.

The stranger was drawing him out of the sun, into the sparse shade of a five-branched palm at the edge of the plaza.

'I am very ill, yes –' he managed finally. 'The heat – my head –'

'Yes. Yes. It is so sad. But look, my friend, the god is coming now.'

He thought at first that some apparition was descending, that Horus or Thoth had come to carry him off to the Land of the Dead. But no, no, that wasn't what the stranger meant at all. A stupefying roar had gone up from the crowd, a bursting swell of incredible noise. The man pointed. He managed to follow the outstretched arm. His vision was blurring again, but he could make out a commotion near the front of the temple, brawny men wearing nothing but strips of blue and gold cloth advancing, wielding whips, people falling back, and then a chariot appearing from somewhere, everything gilded, blindingly bright, falcons on the yoke-pole, a great solar disk above them, winged goddesses on the sides, horned creatures behind; and out of the temple and into the chariot, then, there came a slow portly figure, ornately robed in the stifling heat – the blue crown on his head, the *khepresh*, and the two scepters in his hands, the crook and the flail, and the stiff little false beard strapped to his chin –

The king, it was – it must be – the Pharaoh, getting into the chariot – he has been at some ceremony in the temple, and now he will return to his palace across the river –

Drums and trumpets, and the sound of highpitched things something like oboes. An immense roar. 'Horus!' the crowd was crying now. Ten thousand voices at once, a single throat. 'Horus! Neb-Maat-Re! Life! Health! Strength!'

Neb-Maat-Re. The Pharaoh Amenhotep III, that was what that meant. His coronation name. It was the king himself, yes. Standing there, smiling, acknowledging the crowd, before his very eyes.

'Lord of the Two Lands!' they were shouting. 'Son of Re! Living image of Amon! Mighty one! Benefactor of Egypt! Life! Health! Strength!'

Too much, too much, too much. He was totally overwhelmed by it all. He was thirty-five centuries out of his proper time, a displacement that he had been confident he would be able to comprehend until the moment he found himself actually experiencing it. Now his entire body convulsed in a tremor born of fatigue and confusion and panic. He tottered and desperately grasped the palm tree's rough scaly trunk. The last of his little strength was fleeing under the impact of all this staggering unthinkable reality. Thebes as a living city – Amenhotep III himself, wearing the blue crown – the masked priests, hawk-faced, ibis-faced, dog-faced – the dark mysterious figure of a woman coming out now, surely the queen, taking her place beside the Pharaoh – the chariot beginning to move –

'Life! Health! Strength!'

For the king, maybe. Not for him. How had he ever managed to pass the psychological tests for this mission? He was flunking now. He had been able to fake his way successfully among tougher people all his life, but the truth was coming out at last. His legs were turning to water. His eyes were rolling in his head. They had sent the wrong man for the job: he saw that clearly now. Indeed it was the only thing he could see clearly. He was too complicated, too – *delicate*. They should have sent some stolid unimaginative jock, some prosaic astronaut type, invulnerable to emotion, to the hot dark unreasoning side of life, poetry-free, magic-free, someone who would not become overwhelmed like this by the sight of a fat middle-aged man in a silly costume getting into a Hollywood chariot.

Was it that? Or simply the heat, and the lingering shock of the thirty-five-C jump itself?

'Ah, my friend, my friend,' the dark-eyed stranger was saying, 'I fear you are becoming an Osiris this very minute. It is so sad for you. I will do what I can to help you. I will use my skills. But you must pray, my dear friend. Ask the king to spare your life. Ask the Lady Isis. Ask the mercy of Thoth the Healer, my friend, or you will die as surely as –'

It was the last thing he heard as he pitched forward and crumpled to the ground at the palm tree's base.

CHAPTER TWO

The stranger rested quietly on a bed in the House of Life in the Precinct of Mut that lay just to the south of Ipet-sut, the great temple of Amon, in the baffling jumble of holy buildings that future ages would call Karnak. The pavilion he was in was open to the sky, a simple colonnade; its slim pillars, rising like stems to the swollen lotus-buds at the top, were painted a soothing pink and blue and white. The stranger's eyes were closed and peaceful and his breath was coming slowly and easily, but there was the gleam of fever on his face and his lips were drawn back in an odd grimace, an ugly lopsided smile. Now and again a powerful shudder rippled through his body.

'He will die very soon, I think,' the physician said. His name was Hapu-seneb and he was the one who had been with the stranger when he collapsed outside the Temple of the Southern Harem of Amon.

'No,' said the priestess. 'I think he will live. I am quite sure that he will live.'

The physician made a soft smothered sound of scorn.

But the priestess paid no heed to that. She moved closer to

the bed, which stood high off the floor of the room and sloped noticeably from head to foot. The stranger lay naked on a mattress of cord matting, tightly stretched and covered with cushions, and his head rested on a curving block of wood. He was slender and light-boned, almost feminine in his delicacy, though his lean body was muscular and covered with a thick mat of dark curling hair.

Her hand lightly touched his forehead.

'Very warm,' she said.

'A demon is in him,' said Hapu-seneb. 'There is little hope. He will be an Osiris soon. I think the crocodile of the West has him, or perhaps the rerek-snake is at his heart.'

Now it was the priestess' turn to utter a little skeptical snort.

She was a priestess in the service of Isis, although this was the Precinct of Mut and the entire temple complex was dedicated to Amon; but there was nothing unusual about that. Things overlapped; boundaries were fluid; one god turned easily into another. Isis must be served, even in Amon's temple. The priestess was tall for a woman, and her skin was very pale. She wore a light linen shift that was no more substantial than mist: her breasts showed through, and the dark triangle at her loins. A heavy black wig of natural hair, intricately interwoven in hundreds of tight plaits, covered her shaven scalp.

The stranger was muttering now in his sleep, making harsh congested sounds, a babble of alien words.

'He speaks demon-language,' Hapu-seneb said.

'Shh! I'm trying to hear!'

'You understand the language of demons, do you?'

'Shh!'

She put her ear close by his mouth. Little spurts and freshets of words came from him: babble, delirium, then a pause, then more feverish muttering. Her eyes widened a little as she listened. Her forehead grew furrowed; she tucked her lower lip in, and nibbled it lightly.

'What is he saying, then?' asked Hapu-seneb.

'Words in a foreign language.'

'But you understand them. After all, you're foreign yourself. Is he a countryman of yours?'

'Please,' said the priestess, growing irritated. 'What good are these questions?'

'No good at all,' the physician said. 'Well, I will do what I can to save him, I suppose. Your countryman. If that is what he is.' He brought his equipment with him, his wooden chest of medicines, his pouch of amulets. He gave some thought to selecting an amulet, picking one finally that showed the figure of Amon with four rams' heads, trampling on a crocodile while eight gods adored him in the background. He whispered a spell over it and fastened it to a knotted cord, which he tied to the stranger's kilt. He placed the amulet over the stranger's heart and made magical passes, and said in a deep, impressive tone, 'I am this Osiris here in the West. Osiris knows his day, and if he does not exist in it, then I will not exist in it. I am Re who is with the gods and I will not perish; stand up, Horus, that I may number you among the gods.'

The priestess watched, smiling a little.

The physician said, 'There are other spells I can use.' He closed his eyes a moment and breathed deeply. 'Behind me, crocodile, son of Set!' he intoned. 'Float not with thy tail. Seize not with thy two arms. Open not thy mouth. May the water become a sheet of fire before thee! The charm of thirty-seven gods is in thine eye. Thou art bound to the four bronze pillars of the south, in front of the barge of Re. Stop, crocodile, son of Set! Protect this man, Amon, husband of thy mother!'

'That must be a good spell,' said the priestess. 'See, he's stirring a little. And I think his forehead grows cool.'

'It is one of the most effective spells, yes. But medicines are important too.' The physician began to rummage through the wooden chest, drawing forth little jars, some containing crushed insects, some containing live ones, some holding the powdered dung of powerful animals.

The priestess laid her hand lightly on Hapu-seneb's arm.

'No,' she said. 'No medicines.'

'He needs –'

'What he needs is to rest. I think you should go now.'

'But the powder of the scorpion –'

'Another time, Hapu-seneb.'

'Lady, I am the physician, not you.'

'Yes,' she said gently. 'And a very fine physician you are. And your spells have been very fine also. But I feel Isis in my veins, and the goddess tells me that what will heal this man is sleep, nothing other than sleep.'

'Without medicine he will die, lady. And then Isis will have her Osiris.'

'Go, Hapu-seneb.'

'The oil of serpent, at least –'

'Go.'

The physician scowled and began to say something; but then he converted his anger deftly into a shrug and started to pack up his medical equipment. The priestess was a favorite of the young Prince Amenhotep; everyone knew that. It was perhaps not a good idea to disagree with her too strongly. And if she thought she knew what sort of care this stranger needed better than he did, well –

When Hapu-seneb was gone, the priestess threw some grains of incense on the brazier in the corner of the pavilion and stood for a time staring out into the deepening darkness, breathing deeply and trying to calm herself, for she was not at all calm just now, however she may have seemed to the physician. In the distance she heard chanting. A darkening blue was descending from the sky and changing the river's color. The first stars were appearing overhead. A few fireflies flickered past the tops of the columns. From far away came the mournful sound of the night-trumpet, floating across the water from the royal palace on the west bank.

Well then, she thought.

She considered what had to be done now.

She clapped her hands twice, and two slave-girls came running. To the older and more intelligent one she said, 'Go to the House of Stars which is behind the shrine of Men-Kheper-Re, Eyaseyab, and tell Senmut-Ptah the astronomer to come to me right away. He will tell you that he has important work to do. Say to him that I know that, and want him to come all the same, that it's absolutely essential, an emergency.' The priestess sent the other slave off to fetch cloths steeped in cool water, so that she could bathe the stranger's forehead.

The stranger was still unconscious, but he had stopped babbling now. His face was no longer so rigidly set and the sheen of fever was nearly gone. Perhaps he was simply asleep. The priestess stood above him, frowning.

She leaned close to him and said, 'Can you hear me?'

He shifted about a bit, but his eyes remained closed.

'I am Isis,' she said softly. 'You are Osiris. You are my Osiris. You are the lost Osiris who was cut asunder and restored to life in my care.'

He said something now, indistinctly, muttering in his own language again.

'I am Isis,' she said a second time.

She rested her hand on his shoulder and let it travel down his body, pausing over his heart to feel the steady beating, then lower, and lower still. His loins were cool and soft, but she felt a quickening in them as her fingers lingered. The priestess smiled. Turning away, she picked up the cool cloth that the young slave-girl had brought and lightly mopped his forehead with it. His eyes fluttered open. Had the cool cloth awakened him, she wondered? Or had it been the touch of her hand at the base of his belly a moment before?

He was staring at her.

'How do you feel?' she asked.

'A little better.' He spoke very softly, so that she had to strain to hear him.

He glanced down at his nakedness. She saw the movement of his eyes and draped a strip of cloth that she had not yet moistened across his middle.

'Where am I?'

'The House of Life in the Precinct of Mut. The physician Hapu-seneb found you in the street outside the southern temple and brought you here. I am Nefret. Isis is the one I serve.'

'Am I dying, Nefret?'

'I don't think so.'

'The man who found me said I was. He told me I was about to become Osiris. That means I'm dying, doesn't it?'

'It can mean that. It can mean other things. Hapu-seneb is a very fine physician, but he's not always right. You aren't dying. I think the heat was too much for you, that's all. That and perhaps the strain of your voyage.' She studied him thoughtfully. 'You came a long way?'

He hesitated before replying. 'You can tell, can you?'

'A child could tell. Where are you from?'

Another little pause. A moistening of the lips. 'It's a place called America.'

'That must be very far away.'

'Very.'

'Farther than Syria? Farther than Crete?'

'Farther, yes. Much farther.'

'And your name?' the priestess asked.

'Edward Davis.'

'Ed-ward Da-vis.'

'You pronounce it very well.'

'Edward Davis,' she said again, less awkwardly. 'Is that better?'

'You did it well enough the first time.'

'What language do they speak in the place called America?' she asked.

'English.'

'Not American?'

'Not American, no. English.'

'You were speaking in your English while you were asleep, I think.'

He looked at her. 'Was I?'

'I suppose,' she said. 'How would I know? I heard foreign words, that's all I can tell you. But you speak our language very well, for someone who comes from so far away.'

'Thank you.'

'Very well indeed. You arrived just today, did you?'

'Yes.'

'By the ship that sailed in from Crete?'

'Yes,' he said. 'No. No, not that one. It was a different ship, the one that came from –' He paused again. 'It was the ship from Canada.'

'Canada. Is that near America?'

'Very near, yes.'

'And ships from Canada come here often?'

'Not really. Not very often.'

'Ah,' she said. 'But one came today.'

'Or yesterday. Everything's so confused for me – since I became sick –'

'I understand,' the priestess said. She swabbed his forehead with the cool cloth again. 'Are you hungry?'

'No, not at all.' Then he frowned. Messages seemed to be traveling around inside his body. 'Well, a little.'

'We have some cold roast goose, and some bread. And a little beer. Can you handle that?'

'I could try,' he said.

'We'll bring you some, then.'

The slave-girl who had gone to fetch the astronomer had returned. She was standing just outside the perimeter of the pavilion, waiting. The priestess glanced at her.

'The priest Senmut-Ptah is here, lady. Shall I bring him to you?'

'No. No, I'll go to him. This is Edward-Davis. He was ill, but I think he's recovering. He'd like to have some food, and something to drink.'

'Yes, lady.'

The priestess turned to the stranger again. He was sitting up on the bed now, looking off toward the west, toward the river. Night had fully arrived by this time and the torches had been lit along the west bank promenade, and in the hills where the kings' tombs were. He appeared to be caught up in some enchantment.

'The city is very beautiful at night, yes,' she said.

'I can hardly believe I'm really here.'

'There's no city like it in all the land. How fortunate you are to see it at its greatest.'

'Yes,' he said. 'I know.'

His eyes were shining. He turned to stare at her, and she

knew that he was staring at her body through her filmy gown, back-lit by the torches behind her. She felt exposed and curiously vulnerable, and found herself wishing she was wearing something less revealing. It was a long time since she had last cared about that.

The priestess wondered how old he was. Twenty-five, perhaps? Perhaps even less. Younger than she by a good many years, that much was certain.

She said, 'This is Eyaseyab. She'll bring you food. If you want anything else, just ask her.'

'Are you going?'

'There's someone I have to speak with,' the priestess said.

'And then you'll come back?'

'Later.'

'Not too much later, I hope.'

'Eat. Rest. That's what's important now. Eyaseyab will take care of you.' She smiled and turned away. She could feel his eyes on her as she left the pavilion.

CHAPTER THREE

Senmut-Ptah was waiting for her outside, by the great sphinx that bore the inscription of Tuthmosis III. He was wearing a kilt of scarlet cloth into which golden ibises had been woven, and a tall priestly crown with three long feathers set in it. His shoulders and chest were bare. He was a long-limbed, bony man, very broad through the shoulders, and his features were sharp and powerful, giving him a falcon-face, a Horus-hawk face. Just now he looked angry and impatient.

'You know you've made me miss the rising of the Bull's Thigh,' he said at once, when she appeared. 'The North Star will be past the meridian by the time I –'

'Shh,' she said. 'The North Star won't go anywhere unusual tonight, and the Bull's Thigh will look just the same tomorrow. Walk with me. We have to talk.'

'What about?'

'Walk,' she said. 'We can't talk here. Let's go down toward the Sacred Lake.'

'I don't understand why we can't –'

'*Because we can't*,' she said in a fierce whisper. 'Come on.

Walk with me. The astronomer and the priestess of Isis, out for
a little stroll by starlight.'

'I have important observations that absolutely have to be
made this evening, and –'

'Yes, I know,' she said.

She loathed the all-enveloping obsessive concern with his
astronomical duties that had taken possession of him in recent
years. He was like a machine, now. Or like an insect of some sort,
clicking along busily in his preprogrammed routines. Day and
night preoccupied with his viewing apertures and his transits, his
reflecting bowls, his azimuths and meridians and ascensions, his
sundials and his water-clocks. Once, when the two of them were
new here and first struggling with the terrible challenge of
building lives for themselves in Egypt, he had been aflame with
wonder and eager curiosity and a kind of burning dauntlessness,
but that was all gone now. Nothing seemed to matter to him any
longer except his observations of the stars. Somewhere along the
way a vast leaden indifference had come to engulf all the rest of
him. Why was it so important to him, that absurd compilation of
astronomical data, probably inaccurate and in any case useless?
And where had he misplaced the warmth and passion that had
carried the two of them through all the difficulties they had had to
face in this strange land in earlier days?

He glared at her now as though he would send her to the
Lake of Fire with a single flash of his eyes, if he could. By the
chilly light of the stars his eyes seemed cruel and cold to her,
and his face, sculpted to harshness by the years, had some of
the nightmare look of the gods whose images were engraved on
every wall of every temple. She had once thought he was
handsome, even romantic, but time had made his face and
body gaunt just as it had turned his soul to stone. He was as ugly
as Thoth now, she thought. And as horrid as Set.

But he was the closest thing to an ally that she had in this eternally strange land, unless she counted the prince; and the prince was dangerously unstable, and an Egyptian besides. However much the man who stood before her had changed since he and she had first come to Thebes, he was nevertheless someone of her own kind. She needed him. She couldn't let herself ever forget that.

She slipped her arm through his and tugged him along, through the colonnade that surrounded the Precinct of Mut, down the new avenue that Pharaoh had built, lined by a double row of cobras, and across the field toward the Sacred Lake. When they had gone far enough from the House of Life so that there was no chance the breeze might carry her voice upward to the sick man in the pavilion she said, speaking suddenly in English, 'Someone from downtime showed up in Thebes today, Roger. From Home Era.'

The shift to English was like the throwing of a switch. It was years since she had spoken it, and the effect was immediate and emphatic for her. She felt her former identity, so long suppressed, come leaping forth now from its entombment. Her heart pounded; her breasts rose and fell quickly.

The man who called himself Senmut-Ptah seemed shaken as though by an earthquake. He made a choking sound and pulled himself free of her. Then his icy self-control reasserted itself.

'You can't be serious. And why are you speaking English?'

'Because Egyptian doesn't have the words I need in order to tell you what I have to tell you. And because I wouldn't want anyone who might overhear us to understand.'

'I hate speaking it.'

'I know you do. Speak it anyway.'

'All right. English, then.'

'And I *am* serious.'

'Someone else from downtime is here? Really?'

'Yes. Really.'

The corner of his mouth made a little quirking motion. He was trying to comprehend her news and obviously having a difficult time of it. She had finally broken through that indifference of his. But it had taken something like this to do it.

'His name's Edward Davis. He's very young, very innocent in a charming way. He was staggering around outside Luxor Temple this afternoon right about the time the king was leaving, and he passed out with heatstroke and a bad case of temporal shock practically at Hapu-seneb's feet. Hapu-seneb brought him to me. I've got him in the House of Life this very minute. Eyaseyab's trying to get a little food into him.'

The astronomer stared. His nostrils flickered tensely. She could see him fighting to maintain his poise.

Sullenly he said, 'This is all a fantasy. You're making it up.'

'I wish. He's real.'

'Is he? Is he?'

'I could take you to him right now. You can say hello to him in English and hear what he says.'

'No. No, I don't want to do that.'

'What are you afraid of?'

'I'm not afraid of anything. But if you've got someone from Home Era up there in your temple, the last thing I would want to do is go to him and give him a big happy handshake. The absolutely last thing.'

'Will you believe me without seeing him, then?'

'If I have to.'

'You have to, yes. Why would I want to invent something like this?'

His lips worked, but for a moment no sound came out.

'Yes, why would you?' he said, finally. And then, after another pause: 'When is he from?'

'I don't know, but it's got to be a year pretty close to ours. He told me right flat out that he's from America – what should he care, he must figure the word's just a meaningless noise to me? – and that he came in today or yesterday on a ship from Canada. He started to say he sailed in from Crete, but maybe it occurred to him that I could check up on that. Or maybe he just enjoys telling whoppers. Did you know an Edward Davis when you were in the Service?'

'I don't remember any.'

'Neither do I.'

'He must be later than we are.'

'I suppose. But not much. I'm sure of that.'

The astronomer shrugged. 'He could come from five hundred years after our time, for all we can tell. Isn't that so?'

'He could. But I don't think he does.'

'Intuition?'

'He just doesn't seem to. *Edward Davis.* Is that your idea of a Twenty-Seventh Century name?'

'How would I know what a Twenty-Seventh Century name would sound like?' he asked, his voice rising angrily. By the glimmering light of the torches set in the sconces ringing the Sacred Lake she saw agitation returning to his face. Ordinarily he was as expressionless as a granite statue. She had broken through, all right.

He began to pace rapidly along the perimeter of the lake. She was hard pressed to keep up with him.

Then he turned and looked back at her.

Hoarsely he said, 'What do you think he wants here, Elaine?'

'What do you think he wants? What else would he be doing here but to study Eighteenth Dynasty Egypt? He speaks the language so well that he must be trained in Egyptology. So he's come on the usual kind of preliminary exploration mission, the sort of thing we were going to do in Rome. Did you really believe that nobody was ever going to come here? Did you, Roger?'

'I wanted to believe that.'

She laughed. 'It had to happen sooner or later.'

'They've got five thousand years of Egyptian history to play with. They could have gone to Memphis to watch the pyramids being built. Or to Alexandria to see Antony screwing Cleopatra. Or to the court of Rameses II.'

'They've probably been all those places,' the priestess said. 'But they'd want to come here too. Thebes is a fabulous city. And it's absolutely at its peak right now. It's an obvious destination.'

The man who called himself Senmut-Ptah nodded glumly. He was silent for a time. He walked even faster. He held his shoulders hunched in an odd way and now and then one of them rose abruptly as though he was being swept by a tic.

At length he said, in a new and oddly flat, unresonant tone, a dead man's voice, 'Well, so someone came at long last. And fell right into your lap on his very first day.'

'Was dumped.'

'Whatever. There he is, up there in your temple, not more than five hundred feet away from us. He could have landed anywhere in Thebes and used up his whole time here without ever laying eyes on either of us or having the slightest notion that we're here, and instead somehow he finds his way to you in a single day. How neat that is.'

'He doesn't know anything about me, Roger.'

'Are you sure of that?'

'Positive.'

'You didn't tell him you aren't Egyptian, did you?'

'I didn't tell him anything.'

'Do you think he could have guessed?'

'He doesn't have a clue. He's still groggy from the jump and he thinks I'm a priestess of Isis.'

'You are a priestess of Isis,' the astronomer said.

'Of course I am. But that's all he knows about me.'

'Right. You didn't say a thing. You wouldn't have.' He came to a halt and stood rigidly with his back toward her, staring off toward the Precinct of Amon. There was another long silence. Then he said, his voice still flat and dead, 'Okay. So we've got a young man from Home Era on our hands, and you know what he is, but he doesn't know what you are. Well. Well, well, well. All right: what are we going to do about him, Elaine?'

'Is there any question about that? I have to get rid of him.'

'Get rid? How? What do you mean?'

'Get him out of the temple, is what I mean. Move him along, send him on his way. See to it that he uses up his time in Thebes without finding out anything about us.'

He gave her a long peculiar look. She had no idea what was going on in his mind. He seemed to be cracking apart. He frightened her, reacting to the coming of the visitor as he was, in all these different contradictory ways.

He moistened his lips and said, 'So you don't want to speak to him at all?'

'Speak to him about what?'

The look on his face grew even more strange. She couldn't remember a time when he had ever seemed so disturbed, not even in the first chaotic days after their arrival. 'Anything. The news from Home Era. What's going on in the world. The Service, our friends. He may know some of them. We haven't heard a thing in fifteen years. Aren't you even curious?'

'Of course I am. But the risks —'

'Yes,' he said.

'We've talked about this so many times. What we would do if somebody from down there showed up.'

'Yes.'

'And now that someone actually has –'

'That changes everything, having someone from down there actually arrive here.'

'It doesn't change a thing,' she said cooly. 'You only think it does. I'm amazed, Roger. You said only a couple of minutes ago that revealing yourself to him was the last thing you'd want to do. You aren't seriously suggesting now that we do it, are you?'

He contemplated that.

'Are you?' she asked.

'No,' he said. 'Not seriously. And you don't want to either.'

'Of course I don't. I just want to be left alone to live my life.'

'Well, so do I.'

'Then we can't let him know anything, can we?'

'No.'

'But you're tempted, all of a sudden. I can see that you are. I didn't expect this of you, Roger.'

He looked past her, into the night, as though she were not there at all. He seemed once again to be rebuilding some of his old glacial indifference. But she knew now that it was only a pose. He was more confused than she had ever imagined.

'Maybe I am tempted, just a little,' he said grudgingly. 'Is that so surprising, that the idea should cross my mind? But of course I don't mean it.'

'Of course not.'

'Of course.'

'Good. I'll take care of this, then. I just wanted you to know what was happening. You can go back to your observatory, now. Maybe there's still time to find the North Star tonight. Or whatever it is that you do.'

She realized that somewhere during the conversation she had gone back to speaking Egyptian, and so had he. She wasn't sure when that had been.

CHAPTER FOUR

In the morning the slave-girl Eyaseyab came into the pavilion where he was lying on the sloping bed and said, 'You are awake? You are better? You are strong today?'

He blinked at her. It must be well along in the morning. The sky was like a blue shield above him and the air was already warming toward the midday scorch. He realized that he was awake and that he felt reasonably strong. During the night the worst effects of the shock of his arrival in Eighteenth Dynasty Egypt seemed to have left him. His throat was dry and his stomach felt hollow, but he was probably strong enough to stand.

He swung his legs over the side of the bed and cautiously got up. The flimsy cloth that was covering him fell away, leaving him naked. That was a little strange; but Eyaseyab was just about naked too, as naked as any of the girls in the tomb paintings in the Valley of the Kings, just a little beaded belt around her hips and a tiny loincloth covering the pubic area. Little anklets of blue beads jingled as she moved. She was sixteen or seventeen, he supposed, though it was hard to tell, and she seemed cheerful and healthy and reasonably clean. Her eyes were dark and glossy and so was her hair, and her skin was a pleasing olive color with a hint of red in it and a golden underhue.

She had brought a basin of water and a flask of perfumed oil. Carefully she washed him, in a way that was the nearest thing to being intimate, but wasn't. He suspected that it could be, if he asked. He had never been washed by a woman like this, at least not since he was a child, and it was enticing and unnerving both at once. When she was done washing him she anointed him with the warm, fragrant oil, rubbing it into his chest and back and thighs. That too was new to him, and very strange. She is a slave, he told himself. She's accustomed to doing this. Now and again she giggled. Once her eyes came up to meet his, and he saw provocation in them; but it seemed unthinkable for him to reach for her now, in this open place, in this *temple*. To draw her to him, to *use* her. She is a slave, he told himself. She expects to be used. Which makes it all the more impossible.

She handed him a white kilt and watched without embarrassment as he clambered into it.

'I have brought food,' she said. 'You will eat and then we will go.'

'Go where?'

'To the place where you will live.'

'On the temple grounds?'

'In town,' she said. 'You will not stay here. The priestess Nefret has said I am to take you to a lodging in the town.'

That was upsetting. He had been hoping to stay here, to be taken into the service of the temple in some fashion. He wanted to speak with that serene, mysterious, aloof priestess again; in this profoundly unfamiliar place she had already begun to seem like an island of security and succor. He had felt a strange kind of rapport with her, some curious sort of kinship, and he would gladly have remained in her domain a little longer. But finding some safe nest to hide in, he knew, would not be a useful way of achieving the goals of his mission here.

Eyaseyab went out and returned shortly with a tray of food for him: a bowl of broth, a piece of grilled fish, some flat bread and a few sweet cakes and a little stone pot of dates. It seemed much too much food. Last night he had only been able to nibble at the meat and beer the girl had brought him. But to his surprise his appetite was enormous today; he emptied the broth bowl in gulps, gobbled the dates, went on to the fish and bread and cakes without hesitating. Vaguely he wondered what sort of microbes he might be ingesting. But of course he had been loaded to the brim with antigens before leaving downtime: one whole division of the Service did nothing but immunological research, and travelers setting out for the past went forth well protected, not just against the great obsolete plagues of yesteryear but against the subtlest of intestinal bugs. He probably had been at greater medical risk during his orientation visit to modern Cairo and Luxor than he was here.

'You want more to eat?' she asked him.

'I don't think I should.'

'You should eat, if you're hungry. Here at the temple there's plenty of food.'

He understood what she was telling him. All well and good; but he couldn't pack away a month's worth of eating at a single sitting.

'Come, then,' she said. 'I will take you to your lodging-place.'

They left the temple precinct by a side gate. A dusty unpaved path took them quickly to the river promenade, just a short walk away. The temples were much closer to the Nile than they would be thirty-five centuries later. Millennia of sedimentation had changed the river's course to a startling extent. In this era

the Nile flowed where, in modern-day Luxor, there was a broad
stretch of land covering several blocks, running from the riverfront promenade to the taxi plaza that served the Karnak ruins,
the ticket-booth area, the approach to the avenue of sphinxes at
the temple's first pylon.

She walked swiftly, keeping half a dozen paces in front of
him, never looking back. He watched with amusement the
rhythmic movements of her buttocks. She was heading south
into the bewildering maze that was the city proper.

He could see now why he was so dazed yesterday. Not only
had he had to cope with the shock of temporal displacement far
beyond anything he had ever experienced on his training
jumps, but the city itself was immense and immediately over-
powering. Thebes of the Pharaohs was far bigger than the
modern Luxor that occupied its site, and it hit you with all its
force the moment you set foot in it. Luxor, its splendid ruins
aside, was no more than a small provincial town: a few tourist
hotels, a one-room museum, a little airport, a railway station
and some shops. Thebes was a metropolis. What was the line
from the ILIAD? 'The world's great empress on the Egyptian
plain, that spreads her conquests o'er a thousand states.' Yes.

The general shape of the place was familiar. Like everything
else in Egypt it was strung out along the north-south line of the
Nile. The two ends of the city were anchored by the great temples
he knew as Luxor and Karnak: Luxor at the southern end, where
he had made his appearance yesterday, and the vast complex of
Karnak, where he had spent the night, a mile or so to the north. As
he faced south now the river was on his right, cluttered with
bright-sailed vessels of every size and design, and beyond it,
across the way to the west, were the jagged tawny mountains of
the Valley of the Kings, where the great ones of the land had their
tombs, with a long row of grand imperial palaces stretching

before them in the river plain, Pharaoh's golden house and the dwellings of his family. When he looked the other way he could see, sharp against the cloudless desert sky, the three lofty hills that marked the eastern boundary, and the massive hundred-gated walls that had still been standing in Homer's time.

What was so overwhelming about Thebes was not so much its temples and palaces and all its other sectors of monumental grandeur – though they were impressive enough – as it was the feverish multifariousness of the sprawling streets that occupied the spaces between them. They spread out as far as he could see, a zone of habitation limited only by the river on the one side and the inexorable barrenness of the desert on the other. City planning was an unknown concept here. Incomprehensibly twisting lanes of swarming tenements stood cheek by jowl beside the villas of the rich. Here was a street of filthy little ramshackle shops, squat shanties of mud brick, and just beyond rose a huge wall that concealed cool gardened courtyards, blue pools and sparkling fountains, quiet hallways bedecked with colored frescoes; and just on the far side of that nobleman's grand estate were the tangled alleys of the poor again. The air was so hot that it seemed to be aflame, and a shimmering haze of dust-motes danced constantly in it, however pure the sky might be in the distance. Insects buzzed unceasingly, flies and locusts and beetles making angry, ominous sounds as they whizzed past, and animals browsed casually in the streets as though they owned them. The smoke of a hundred thousand cooking-fires rose high; the smell of meat grilling on spits and fish frying in oil was everywhere. And a steady pounding of traffic was moving in all directions at once through the narrow, congested streets, the nobles in their chariots or litters, ox-carts carrying produce to the markets, nearly naked slaves jogging along beneath huge mounds of neatly wrapped bundles, donkeys staggering under untidier loads half the size of pyramids, children underfoot, vendors of pots and utensils hauling their wagons, everybody yelling, laughing, bickering, singing, hailing friends with loud whoops. He had been in big exotic cities before – Hong Kong, Honolulu, maddening gigantic Cairo itself – but even they, with all their smoke-belching trucks and autos and motorbikes, were no match for the wondrous chaos of Thebes. This was a disorder beyond anything he had ever experienced: indeed, beyond anything he had ever imagined.

They were near the southern temple now. He recognized the plaza where he had collapsed the day before. But abruptly Eyaseyab turned toward the river and led him down a flight of stone steps into a waterfront quarter that had not been visible from above, where squalid taverns and little smoky food-kiosks huddled in a cluster beside a long stone wharf.

A flat barge crowded with people was waiting at the wharf, and a burly man who seemed obviously to be an overseer was waving his arms and crying out something unintelligible in thick, guttural tones.

'It's going to leave,' Eyaseyab said. 'Quick, let's get on board.'

'Where are we going?'

'To the other side.'

He stared at her blankly. 'You said I'd be lodging in town.'

'It is also the town over there. You will be lodging near the place where you will work. The priestess has arranged everything. You are a very lucky man, Edward-Davis.'

'I don't understand. What sort of work?'

'With the embalmers,' the girl said. 'You will be apprentice in the House of Purification, in the City of the Dead.' She tugged at his wrist. 'Come quickly! If we miss the ferry, there won't be another one going across for an hour.'

Too astonished to protest, he stumbled on board after her. Almost at once, the overseer bellowed a command and slaves along the quayside tugged on the ropes that tied the barge down, pulling them free of the bollards that held them. A huge man wielding an enormous pole pushed the vessel loose and it drifted out into the channel of the Nile. The great red and yellow sails scooped up such breeze as was there for the scooping. The lunatic bustle of Thebes receded swiftly behind them. He stared back at it in dismay.

An embalmer, in the City of the Dead?

A lodging-place on the wrong side of the river?

Some of yesterday's confusion and panic began to surface in him again. He looked toward the distant western shore. His assignment here was difficult enough as it was; but how was he supposed to carry it out while living over there in the mortuary village? Presumably the two people he had come here to find were living in Thebes proper, if they were here at all. He had expected to circulate in the city, to ask questions and generally sniff about in search of unusual strangers, to pursue whatever clues to their whereabouts he might discover. But the priestess, in her great kindness, had essentially exiled him from the place where he had to be. Now he would have to steal time from his work – whatever that was going to be! – and get himself somehow back to the main part of Thebes every day, or as often as he could arrange it, if he was going to carry out his little Sherlock Holmes operation. It was a complication he hadn't anticipated.

In the crush of passengers aboard the greatly overcrowded ferry, the slave-girl was jammed right up against him. He found himself enjoying the contact. But he wondered how often one of these boats foundered and sank. He thought of the crocodiles that still inhabited the Nile in this era.

She laughed and said, 'It is too many people, yes?'

'Yes. Many too many.'

'It's always this busy this time. Better to go early, but you were sleeping.'

'Do the ferries run all day?'

'All day, yes, and less often in the night. Everyone uses them. You are still feeling all right, Edward-Davis?'

'Yes,' he said. He let his hands rest on her bare shoulders. 'Fine.' For a moment he found himself wondering what he was going to use to pay the ferry fare; and then he remembered that this entire empire managed somehow to function without any sort of cash. All transactions involving goods or services were done by barter, and by a system of exchange that used weights and spirals of copper as units of currency, but only in the abstract: workers were paid in measures of grain or flasks of oil that could be traded for other necessities, and more complex sales and purchases were handled by bookkeeping entries, not by the exchange of actual metal. The ferries, most likely, were free of charge, provided by the government by way of offering some return on the labor-taxes that everyone paid.

The ferry wallowed westward across the green sluggish river. The east bank was no more now than a shadowy line on the horizon, with the lofty walls and columns of the two temple compounds the only discernible individual features. On the rapidly approaching western shore he could see now another many-streeted tangle of low mud-brick buildings, though not nearly as congested as the very much larger one across the way, and a towering row of dusty-leaved palm trees just behind the town as a sort of line of demarcation cutting it off from the emptiness beyond. Further in the distance was the sandy bosom of the western desert, rising gradually toward the bleak bare hills on the horizon.

At the quay-side Eyaseyab spoke briefly with a man in a soiled, ragged kilt, apparently to ask directions. They seemed to know each other; they grinned warmly, exchanged a quick handclasp, traded a quip or two. Davis felt an odd, unexpected pang of jealousy as he watched them. The man turned and pointed toward the left: Davis saw as he swung around that his face was terribly scarred and he had only one eye.

'My brother,' Eyaseyab said, coming back toward him. 'He belongs to the ferry-master. We go this way.'

'Was he injured in battle?'

She looked baffled a moment. 'His face? Oh, no, he is no soldier. He ran away once, when he was a boy, and slept in the desert one night, and there was an animal. He says a lion, but a jackal, I think. Come, please.'

They plunged into the City of the Dead, Eyaseyab once more going first and leaving him to trudge along behind, keeping his eyes trained on the tapering glossy wedge of her bare back. On every side the industry of death was operating at full throttle. Here was a street of coffin-makers, and here were artisans assembling funerary furniture in open-fronted arcades, and in another street sculptors were at work polishing memorial statues. A showroom displayed gilded mummy-cases in a startling range of sizes, some no bigger than a cat might need, others enormous and ornate. Silent priests with shaven heads moved solemnly through the busy, crowded streets like wraiths. Now and again Davis caught a whiff of some acrid fumes; embalming fluids, he supposed.

The district where the workers lived was only a short distance behind the main commercial area, but the layout of the village was so confusing that Eyaseyab had to ask directions twice more before she delivered him to his new lodging-place. It was a cave-like warren of dark little mud-walled rooms lopsidedly arranged in a U-shaped curve around a sandy courtyard. Misery Motel, Davis thought. A florid, beefy man named Pewero presided over it. The place was almost comically dismal, filthy and dank and reeking of urine, but even so it had its own proud little garden, one dusty acacia tree and one weary and practically leafless sycamore.

'You will take your meals here,' Eyaseyab explained. 'They are supplied by the House of Purification. There will be beer if you want it, but no wine. Check your room for scorpions before you go to sleep. On this side of the river they are very common.'

'I'll remember that,' Davis said.

She stood waiting for a moment at the door to his little cubicle as though expecting something from him. But of course he had nothing to offer her.

Was that what she wanted, though? A gift? Perhaps that look of expectation meant something else.

'Stay with me this afternoon,' he said impulsively.

She smiled almost demurely. 'The priestess expects me back. There is much work to do.'

'Tonight, then? Can you come back?'

'I can do that, yes,' she said. There wasn't much likelihood of it in her tone. She touched his cheek pleasantly. 'Edward-Davis. What an odd name that is, Edward-Davis. Does everyone in your country have such odd names?'

'Even worse,' he said.

She nodded. Perhaps that was the limit of her curiosity.

He watched her from his doorway as she went down the dusty path. Her slender back, her bare plump buttocks, suddenly seemed almost infinitely appealing to him. But she turned the corner and was gone. I will never see her again, he thought; and he felt himself plummeting without warning into an abyss of loneliness and something approaching terror as he looked back into the dark little hole of a room that was his new home in this strange land.

You wanted this, he told himself.

You volunteered for this. Going back to find a couple of Service people who hadn't come back from a mission was only the pretext, the excuse. What you wanted was to experience the real Egypt. Well, kid, here's the real Egypt, and welcome to it!

He wondered what he was supposed to do next. Report for work? Where? To whom?

Pewero said, 'In the morning. Go with them, when they leave.'

'Who?'

But Pewero had already lost interest in him.

He made his way back through the confusion that was the village, staring about him in wonder at the frantic intensity of it all. He had known, of course, that to an Egyptian death was the most important part of life, the beginning of one's true existence, one's long residence in eternity: but still it was astonishing to see these hordes of men hard at work, turning out a seemingly endless stream of coffins, scrolls, grave-goods, carvings. It was like a gigantic factory. Death was big business in this country. A dozen guilds were at work here. Only the embalmers were not to be seen, though he suspected their workshops would not be far away; but doubtless they kept to one side, in some quieter quarter, out of respect for the corpses over whom they toiled. The dead here were an active and ever-present part of the population, after all. Their sensibilities had to be considered.

He wandered down toward the river and stood by the quay for a while, looking for crocodiles. There didn't seem to be any here, only long ugly fish. Unexpectedly he felt calmness settle over him. He was growing accustomed to the heat; he barely heard the noise of the town. The river, even though at low ebb, was strikingly beautiful, a great smooth green ribbon coming out of the inconceivably remote south and vanishing serenely into the unimaginable north, an elemental force cutting through the desert like the will of God. But it stank of decay; he was astounded, standing by it, to see what was unmistakably a dead body go floating by, perhaps a hundred yards out from the bank. No mummifying for that one, no tomb, no eternal life. A beggar, he supposed, an outcast, the merest debris of society: yet what thoughts had gone through his mind at the last moment, knowing as he did that for him death was the end of everything and not the grand beginning?

A trick of the sunlight turned the muddy banks to gold. The corpse drifted past and the river was beautiful again. When Davis returned to the lodging-house, four men were squatting outside, roasting strips of fish over a charcoal fire. They offered him one, asking him no questions, and gave him a little mug of warm rancid beer. He was one of them, the new apprentice. Perhaps they noticed that his features were those of a foreigner and his accent was an odd one, perhaps not. They were incurious, and why not? Their lives were heading nowhere. They understood that he was as unimportant as they were. Important men did not become apprentices in the House of Purification. The priestess Nefret, meaning to do well by the stranger, had buried him in the obscurity of the most menial of labor over here.

It was going to be a long thirty days, he thought. Here in the real Egypt.

To his utter amazement Eyaseyab appeared in his doorway not long after dark as he sat somberly staring at nothing in particular.

'Edward-Davis,' she said, grinning.
'You? But –'
'I said I would be back.'
So at least there would be some consolations.

CHAPTER FIVE

The real Egypt got even realer, much too real, in the days immediately following.

On the first morning he followed the other men of his little mud tenement when they set out for work soon after sunrise. Silently they marched single file through the rapidly awakening City of the Dead, past the residential district and out a short way into the fringe of the desert. The line of demarcation was unmistakable: no transitional zone, but rather two utterly different worlds butting up against each other, fertile humus and green vegetation and the coolness of the river air on one side, and, on the other, arid sand and rock and the blast-furnace heat of the realm of the dead, striking with the force of a punch even this early in the day. The dawn breeze brought him the briny smell of the embalmers' chemicals, far more pungent than it had been the night before.

And then he saw it, not any kind of house at all but a raggle-taggle pseudo-village, scores of flimsy little booths made of sheets of cloth tacked together in frameworks of wooden struts. It was spread out like a Gypsy encampment over a strip of the desert plain that was probably a thousand yards long and fifty yards or so deep. As he watched, workmen began disassembling a booth not far from him, revealing the workshop within: soiled and wadded cloths, mounds of damp sawdust, rows of phials and flasks and unpainted pottery jars, racks of fearsome-looking tools, a scattering of discarded bandages, and, in the center of the room, a ponderous rectangular table made of four huge wooden butcher's-blocks. The workmen were carefully packing everything up, sweeping the sawdust into large jars, stuffing the cloths in on top, gathering all the tools and chemicals together and putting them in elegant wooden satchels. He thought he understood. The job was finished here; the dead man had gone to his grave; now the booth where his body had lain for the seventy days of his mummification was being dismantled and every scrap, every bit of cloth, every stray hair, was being taken away lest it fall into the hands of some enemy of his who might use it against him in an enchantment. All these booths were temporary things. Each had been constructed for a specific occupant, and it was taken down when he had been safely seen into the next world.

He looked about in wonder. The great work of preparing the dead for the glorious afterlife was proceeding with awesome alacrity on all sides.

He had studied the process, naturally. He had studied every aspect of Egyptian life while preparing for this mission: they had poured it into him, hypnogogic training day and night, a torrent of facts, an electronic encyclopedia engraved on his mind. He knew how they drew the brain out through the nostrils with an iron hook and squirted chemicals in to dissolve whatever remained. How they made an incision in the left flank through which to remove the entrails for their separate interment in stone jars. The cleansing and scouring of the body, the washing of it in palm-wine; the packing of the interior cavity with myrrh and cassia and other aromatics; the many days of curing in a tub of dry natron to purge the body of all putrefying matter, the thirsty salts devouring every drop of the body's moisture, leaving it as hard as wood. The coating of the skin with a carapace of resinous paste. And then the bandaging, the body enveloped in its protective layers of cloth, the hundreds of yards of fine linen so carefully wrapped, each finger and toe individually, thimbles covering the nails to keep them in place, the pouring of unguents, the reciting of prayers and the uttering of magic formulas –

But still, to see it all happening right in front of him – to *smell* it happening –

Someone whacked him on the back.

'Move along, you! Get to work!'

He stumbled and nearly fell.

'Yes – sir –'

Work? Where was he supposed to work? What did they want him to do?

He drifted as though in a dream toward a nearby booth. Its linen door was folded back, half open, and he could see figures moving about within. A naked body lay face down on the great wooden table. Above it stood two figures out of some terrifying dream, men in golden kilts whose heads were concealed by dark Anubis masks – the dog-faced god, the black god of death, tapered narrow ears rising high, dainty pointed muzzles projecting half a foot. These must be the embalmers themselves, members of the secret hereditary guild. A priest stood to one side, droning prayers. There were three other men in the booth, maskless and dressed only in loincloths, handing tools back and forth in response to brief harsh commands. Would an apprentice be useful here? He took a deep breath and went in.

'More oil,' one of the men in loincloths said to him at once, brusquely thrusting a huge sweet-smelling red jar into his arms.

He nodded and backed out of the booth, and looked about in perplexity. An overseer glowered at him. He avoided making eye contact and turned away, trudging up the path as though he knew where he was going. But he hesitated to ask. At any moment, he thought, he would be recognized as an outsider, an impious interloper with no business here. Overseers would take him by the scruff of the neck and carry him to the river – toss him in to provide the crocodiles with breakfast –

Toward him came a boy of thirteen or fourteen, tottering under an immense roll of bandages. The boy, at least, didn't seem to pose a threat. Davis took up a position in the middle of the path, deliberately blocking it. The boy shot him an angry glance and gestured furiously with his head, wordlessly telling him to move aside.

Davis said, 'I need to get some more oil.'

'Then get more oil,' the boy said. 'You're standing in my way.'

'I'm new. I don't know where to go.'

'Fool,' the boy said in disgust. Then he softened a little. 'Cedar oil, is it?'

'Yes,' said Davis, hoping he was right.

'Over there.' The boy nodded toward the left. 'Now get out of the path.'

He saw a dispensing station of some sort where an old withered man, as parched as a mummy himself, was dispensing a dark fluid from a clay jar nearly as tall as he was. A line of workmen stood before it. Davis waited his turn and presented the jar, and the old man ladled the new supply in, splashing it about so liberally that Davis' arms and chest were covered with it.

'You took your time about it,' grunted one of the men in the booth, relieving him of the jar.

'Sorry.'

'Start loading those pipes, will you?'

They were tubes – syringes of a sort – stacked on the floor of the booth. It took a moment for Davis to figure out how they worked; but then he got the knack of it and began filling them with oil and handing them up to the other men, who passed them along to the Anubis-headed embalmers. Who deftly unloaded them into the corpse on the table through the anus.

What was taking place here, he realized, was a bargain-rate mummification. No incisions had been made in this man, no internal organs withdrawn. They were simply pumping him full of a powerful solvent that would leach away the bowels. Then they would sew him up and cover him with natron to dry him out while the oil inside did its work; and when the prescribed number of days had elapsed, they would cut the stitches and let the oil out and send the new Osiris to his final resting-place. There was a cheaper kind of mummification yet, Davis knew, in which they dispensed even with the cedar oil, and simply treated the corpse with natron until it was properly dry. He wondered whether those who were given such skimpy treat-ment could hope to live forever in the afterlife also, and ride through the heavens with the gods on the boat of the sun. No doubt they did. He began to see why these Egyptians were all so exuberant. So long as they could give their bodies some sort of preparation for the life to come, they were guaranteed virtual immortality, not only the kings but even the humble merchants, the boatmen, the peasants. No reason to be bitter about one's lot in life: better times were coming, and they would endure forever.

His first day in the necropolis seemed to endure forever also. He drifted from booth to booth, filling in wherever he seemed to be needed, doing whatever they seemed to want him to do.

The day was a fever-dream of intestines and stinks, of salts and oils, of dead bodies lying like meat on wooden blocks. It astonished him that death had undone so many this day in Thebes. But then he reminded himself that this wasn't only one day's crop; the mummification process lasted a couple of months and there were bodies here in all stages of preparation, ranging from those who had just undergone their preliminary cleaning to those who had attained the requisite level of desiccation and were ready to be carried to their resting places in the hills. Several times during the day new deads arrived at the necropolis, borne on litters with their friends and members of their family grieving by their sides and parties of professional mourners, women with bare breasts and disheveled hair, sobbing along behind. Davis helped to construct the embalmers' booth for one of these new arrivals; it was the most pleasing thing he had done all day, swift, neat, clean work. In late afternoon just as the sky was beginning to redden behind the jagged hills he witnessed the other end of the process, the departure of a funeral cortege toward the actual place of burial. It must have been someone of note who had died, for the procession was extensive: first servants carrying intricately carved alabaster jars that very likely contained foodstuffs and perfumed oils for the use of the dead man in the next world, and then men bearing heavy, ornately decorated wooden chests that must hold his fine clothing, his prized possessions, all the treasure that he was taking with him to the afterlife; and after them came the four jars of polished stone containing the deceased's embalmed viscera, carried upon a sled. A priest was alongside, chanting. The mummy itself was next, handsomely encased and resting on a couch beneath a canopy, all mounted upon another sled, this one gilded, with ebony runners. Four more priests accompanied it; and then the family and friends, not grieving now, but looking calm and rather proud of the fine show of which they were a part. In the rear once again were the professional mourners, a dozen of them wailing desperately and beating their breasts, each of them every bit as distraught as though it was her own husband or father who had been taken from her that very morning.

The procession passed through the embalmers' village and out the far side, heading toward the looming cliffs just to the west. It was grand enough, Davis thought, for a vizier, a judge, a high priest, at the very least. A prince, perhaps.

'Who's being carried there, do you know?' Davis asked the man by his side.

'Mahu, I think. Overseer of the royal granaries, he was.'

'A rich man?'

'Rich? Mahu? No, not really. Too honest, Mahu was.'

Davis stared at the retreating cortege. How splendid it looked against the light of the setting sun! And this was only a bureaucrat's funeral. He wondered what a nobleman's must be like, or a king's.

He had seen some of the royal tombs during his orientation visit to Luxor, those haunting surreal catacombs endlessly decorated with the bewildering profuse mysteries of the Book of Gates and the Book of the Night and the Book of the Underworld, and he had seen smaller but jollier tombs of nobles and high officials as well. Had Mahu's tomb survived to come before the eyes of modern-day archaeologists and tourists? He had no idea. Perhaps it had, but no one cared. Mahu had been an honest man; his tomb must not have compared with those of the great lords.

The great ones, Davis already knew, did not undergo their mummifications amidst the vulgar hubbub of the embalmers' village. For them the booths were set up closer to the tomb sites, well away from the stares of the curious; and they were guarded day and night until they were at last safely packed away underground amidst all their worldly wealth. Which had made no difference in the long run, for all the tombs had been plundered eventually, all but insignificant Tut-ankh-Amon's, and even his had been broken into a couple of times, though the thieves had left most of the treasure behind. But the mummies themselves, some of them, had survived. In the Cairo Museum Davis had looked upon the actual face of Rameses the Great, stern and fierce, ninety years old and still outraged by the idea of dying: he was one who had meant to stay on the throne forever, to have his afterlife and his first life at the same time. *My name is Ozymandias, King of Kings. Look on my works, ye mighty, and despair!* And – shivering now – he realized that he had seen Amenhotep III's mummy in the museum also, the mortal remains of the plump sleek-cheeked man whom he had watched, only two days before, as he came forth from Luxor Temple, a living god, happy and well, becrowned and bejeweled, who had clambered into his royal chariot and driven off while his adoring subjects cheered – *Life! Health! Strength!*

Davis trembled. He had been with the Service for five years; and it seemed to him that it was only in this moment that the full power of the meaning of being able to travel in time came home to him. The awesome privilege, the utter magnificence of having the gates of the past rolled back for him. For him!

I must not have much of an imagination, he thought.

'You! Standing and watching!'

A whip came out of somewhere and coiled around his bare shoulders like a fiery cobra.

He turned. An overseer was laughing at him.

'Work to do. Who do you think you are?'

Work, yes. Soiled rags to collect. Blood-stained rags, leftover salts, broken pots. He entered one booth where a fat man lay on his back, staring through empty sockets at the darkening sky. A vivid line of stitches crossed his belly, holding in the packing of myrrh and cassia. The fat man's jaw sagged in the stupefaction of death. All those fine dinners: what did they matter now? *Look on my works, ye mighty!* On a table in the adjoining booth was a woman, a girl, perhaps fifteen or twenty years old, small-breasted and slender. She had just arrived; the craftsmen of the necropolis had not yet begun their work on her. The elaborate wig of dense midnight-blue hair that she had worn in life sat beside her on the table. Her shaven skull was like porcelain. Her fingernails and toenails were dyed dark red with henna and there was blue-green eye-paint around her sightless eyes. A gold bracelet encircled her lovely arm: maybe she had worn it since a child and it could no longer be removed. Her nakedness was heartbreaking. He felt an impulse to cover it. But he moved on, only remotely aware now of the odor of death and of the chemicals of the embalmers. It was dark now. The Anubis-masked embalmers had gone home. His body ached everywhere from his day's work, and he knew the pain was just beginning. He was stained with oils and assorted aromatics. His shoulders burned from the sting of the over-seer's whip. The real Egypt, all right. Seen from the underside. Could he leave now, or would he be whipped again? No, no, all the workers were leaving. Night-guards were coming on duty; one of them glanced at him and made a jerking motion with his head, telling him to get out, go back to his village, call it a day.

He had grilled fish for dinner again, and rancid beer.

Later he sat up, staring at the impossibly brilliant stars in the astonishingly clear sky, and wondered whether Eyaseyab would come to him again. But why should she? What was he to her? A comet in the night, a random visitor to whom she had granted a moment of kindness. After a time he went inside his foul little cubicle and lay down on the straw that was his bed.

I must get back across the river, he told himself. I need to find –

And sleep came up in the midst of the thought and took him like a bandit who had thrown a heavy hood over his head.

CHAPTER SIX

Four days went by very much like the first one, in a dreamlike haze of hard work and overmastering strangeness.

He knew he needed to get out of this place, that he had to go back across the river and set about the search for the two missing members of the Service whose trajectories had gone astray and who – so the calculations indicated – were somewhere hereabouts. And, while he was at it, take in as much as he could of mighty Thebes. He had no business settling down like this in the necropolis. He had been sent here in part to rescue the vanished Roger Lehman and Elaine Sandburg, and in part as a scholar of sorts who had been trained to observe and report on one of the most glorious of all ancient cities; and although it might be useful for him to be learning the things that he was concerning the village of the embalmers, it was definitely time to move along. He owed that much to Sandburg, to Lehman, to the Service. Yet a curious trance-like lassitude held him. He sensed that the exhaustion of the day of his arrival had never really lifted from him. He had *seemed* to recover, he had gone past that frightening stage of dizziness and fainting, he could even cope with the hellish heat, he was able to put in a full working day at manual labor, some of it quite nasty; but in truth he realized that he had drawn back into this awful place as a kind of refuge and he was unable to muster the energy to get out and get on with his real work.

On the fourth night Eyaseyab unexpectedly returned. He had given up all hope of her.

When she appeared, trudging into the compound wearing little more than a shawl over her shoulders, the other men looked enviously at him, with a certain puzzlement and awe in their expressions. A slave-girl of the temple, a young and pretty one at that, coming to see him! Why, the stranger must not be as stupid as he seems. Or else he has some other merit that must not be readily apparent.

He wondered about it himself. And decided that he must seem elegant and exotic to her, courtly, even, a man with manners far beyond those of the class to which he obviously belonged. He was a luxury to her.

As she lay beside him that night she said, 'You like it here? You are doing well?'

'Very well.'

'You work hard, you will rise in the House. Perhaps your children will be embalmers, even.'

He brought his hand up her side and cupped her breast.

'Children? What children?'

'Of course you will have children.'

What was she talking about? The children that she would bear for him?

'Even if I did,' he said, 'how could they become embalmers? Isn't the guild hereditary?'

'You could marry an embalmer's daughter,' she told him. 'They would have you. You are very handsome. You are very intelligent. An embalmer's daughter would do well to be married to a man like you. You could choose the best of the daughters of the House of Purification. And then your wife's father would bring your children into the guild. How fine that would be for you and all your descendants!'

'Yes,' he said dispiritedly.

The conversation was drifting into strange places. He imagined himself sitting at his dining-room table at the head of his clan, with his sons around him, each one wearing his little Anubis mask, gravely discussing the fine points of embalming with his father-in-law. How fine that would be, yes.

He was struck by the realization that Eyaseyab seemed to expect him to remain in the House of Purification for the rest of his life. A wonderful career opportunity, evidently. And of course she had automatically ruled herself out as a potential mate for him. She was a slave; he was a free man, and handsome and intelligent besides. Not for the likes of her. Perhaps slaves weren't allowed to marry. He was a divertissement for her, a novelty item who would pass swiftly through her life – like a comet, yes, the image was a good one – and disappear.

To distract himself he stroked the plump pleasant spheroid of her breast. But it had lost all erotic charge for him. It was flesh, only flesh. He had a sudden horrifying vision of good-hearted Eyaseyab lying face-up on a wooden table in one of the booths of the House of Purification. But no, no, they wouldn't send a slave's body there. What did they do with them, throw them into the Nile?

Abruptly he said, 'In the morning I want to go across the river. I have to see the priestess Nefret again.'

'Oh, no. That would be impossible.'

'You can get me into the temple.'

'The priestess sees no one from outside.'

'Nevertheless,' he said. 'Do it for me. Tell her it's urgent, tell her that Edward-Davis has important business with her.' He hovered over her in the darkness. His thumb lightly caressed her nipple, which began to grow rigid again. In a low voice he said, 'Tell her that Edward-Davis is in truth an ambassador from a foreign land, and needs to speak with her about highly significant matters.'

She began to laugh. She wriggled and slipped her knee between his thighs and began to slide it back and forth.

'I'm serious,' he said.

'Yes. Of course you are. Now stop talking and put it in me the way you do so well.'

'Eyaseyab –'

'Like this.'

'I want you – to talk – to the priestess –'

'Shh.'

'Eyaseyab.'

'Yes. Yes. Good. Oh, you are Amon! You are Min! Oh, yes! Yes, Edward-Davis! Oh – don't stop –'

Was he supposed to include this in his report? he wondered.

The Service had no vow of chastity. But some things were none of their business.

'You are Amon! You are Min!'

She was slippery with sweat in the heat of the night. He said no more to her about going across the river to see the priestess, and eventually they slept.

But when he heard her up and moving about the room a few hours later, getting her things together, he reached out, hooked his finger into her anklet in the darkness, and whispered, 'Wait for me. I'm coming with you.'

'You mustn't!' She sounded frightened.

'I need to see the priestess.'

She seemed baffled by his insistent need to do what could not be done. But in the end she yielded: she was a slave, after all, accustomed to obeying. As they crossed the Nile on the early-morning ferry she still appeared tense and apprehensive, but he stroked her soft shoulders and she grew calm. The river at sunrise was glorious, a streak of polished turquoise running between the two lion-colored strips of land. Two little elongated puffs of cloud were drifting above the western hills and the early light turned them to pennants of flame. He saw white ibises clustering in the sycamore trees along the shore.

They entered the temple grounds through the side gate by which they had left, nearly a week before. A burly pockmarked guard scowled at him as he passed through, but he kept his head up and moved as though he belonged there. On the steps of the House of Life Eyaseyab paused and said, 'You wait here. I will see what can be managed.'

'No, don't leave me here. Take me inside with —'

Too late. She was gone. He prowled outside the building, uneasily looking around. But no one seemed to care that he was there. He studied a pair of elegant stone cobras, one wearing the red crown of Lower Egypt, the other wearing the white crown of the southern kingdom. He dug about in the sandy soil with the tip of his big toe, and unearthed a superb scarab of blue faience that any museum would have been proud to own. He touched his hand wonderingly to the flawlessly executed and brightly painted bas-relief that was carved along the wall: Pharaoh before the gods, Isis to his left, Osiris to the right, Thoth and Horus in the background, the ibis-head and the hawk.

Egypt. Egypt. Egypt.

He had dreamed all his life of coming here. And here he was. Well ahead of normal Service schedule for such a major mission, and all because of Elaine Sandburg and Roger Lehman.

'I'm not so sure I want to find out what they've turned into,' Charlie Farhad had told him, explaining why he had refused to take on the assignment. 'The past's a weird place. It can make you pretty weird yourself, if you stay in it long enough.'

'They've only been there a year and a half.'

'Not necessarily,' Farhad had said. 'Think about it.'

Sandburg and Lehman had been heading for the Rome of Tiberius, a ninety-day reconnaissance. But they had missed their return rendezvous and an analysis of the field spectrum indicated some serious anomalies – i.e., an overshoot. How much of an overshoot had taken almost a year to calculate. A lot of algorithmic massage produced the conclusion that instead of landing in 32 A.D. they had plopped down at least thirteen centuries earlier and a goodly distance to the east: Eighteenth Dynasty Egypt, the calculations indicated. 'Poor Roger,' Charlie Farhad said. 'He was so damned proud of his Latin, too. Won't do him a fucking bit of good now, will it?' The algorithm was a murky one; the calculation was only probabilistic. Sandburg and Lehman might have landed right on top of the Nile, or they could have turned up in some merciless corner of the Arabian desert. The high-probability line said Thebes. The most likely year was 1390 B.C., but the time range was plus or minus ten years. Not a hope in hell of finding them again, right? Nevertheless an attempt to rescue them had to be made, but none of the veteran time-jockeys wanted to touch it. That was their privilege. They hinted darkly about serious risk and the considerable unlikelihood of success. And in any case they had their own projects to worry about.

Davis heard what they had to say, but in the end he had volunteered anyway. Fools rush in, et cetera. He hadn't known

Sandburg and Lehman at all: the Service was a big operation, and he was pretty far down in junior staff. So he wasn't doing it out of friendship. He took the job on partly because he was in love with the idea of experiencing Egypt in the prime of its greatness, partly because he was young enough still to see something romantic as well as useful to his career about being a hero, and partly because his own real-time life had taken some nasty turns lately – a collapsed romance, a bitter unexpected parting – and he was willing enough to go ricocheting off thirty-five centuries regardless of the risks. And so he had. And here he was.

Eyaseyab appeared at the head of the stairs and beckoned to him.

'The prince is with her. But he will be leaving soon.'

'The prince?'

'Pharaoh's son, yes. The young Amenhotep.' A mischievous look came into the slave-girl's eyes. 'He is Nefret's brother.'

Davis was bewildered by that for a moment. Then he recognized the idiom. This was an incestuous land: Eyaseyab meant that the priestess and the prince were lovers. A tingle of awe traveled quickly along his spine. She was talking about the fourth Amenhotep, the future Pharaoh Akhnaten, he who would in another few years attempt to overthrow the old gods of Egypt and install a new cult of solar worship that had only a single deity. Akhnaten? Could it be? Up there now, just a hundred feet away, at this moment caressing the priestess Nefret? Davis shook his head in wonder. This was like standing in the plaza and watching Pharaoh himself come out of the temple. He had expected to lurk around the periphery of history here, not to be thrust right into the heart of it. That he was seeing these people in the flesh was remarkable, but not entirely pleasing. It cheapened things, in a way, to be running into actual major historical figures; it made it all seem too much like a movie. But at least it was a well-done movie. The producers hadn't spared any expense.

'Is that him?' Davis asked.

Of course it was. The tingle returned, redoubled. A figure had appeared on the portico of the House of Life. He gaped at it: a very peculiar figure indeed, a slender young man in a loose pleated linen robe with wide sleeves trimmed with blue bows. The upper half of his body seemed frail, but from the waist down he was fleshy, thick-bodied, soft-bellied. A long jutting jaw, a narrow head, full lips: an odd-looking mysterious face. He was instantly recognizable. Only a few weeks before Davis had peered wonder-struck at the four giant statues of him in the Amarna gallery at the far end of the ground floor at the Cairo Museum. Now here was the man himself.

Here and gone. He smiled at Davis in an eerie otherworldly way as if to say, *Yes, you know who I am and I know who you are*, and went quickly down the back steps of the temple's podium. A litter must have been waiting for him there. Davis watched as he was borne away.

'Now,' he said to Eyaseyab, forcing himself to snap from his trance. 'Did you tell the priestess I'm here?'

'Yes. She says no. She says she will not see you.'

'Go back inside. Ask her again.'

'She seemed angry that you are here. She seemed very annoyed. *Very* annoyed.'

'Tell her that it's a matter of life and death.'

'It will do no good.'

'Tell her. Tell her that I'm here and it's extremely important that I get to see her. Lives are at stake, the lives of good, innocent people. Remind her who I am.'

'She knows who you are.'

'Remind her. Edward-Davis, the man from America.'

'A-meri-ca.'

'America, yes.'

She trotted up the stairs again. Some moments passed, and then a few more. And then Eyaseyab returned, eyes wide with amazement, face ruddy and bright with surprise and chagrin.

'Nefret will see you!'

'I knew she would.'

'You must be very important!'

'Yes,' he said. 'I am.'

The priestess was waiting for him in an antechamber. As before, she was wearing a filmy gown, casually revealing in what he was coming to regard as the usual Egyptian way; but she was more splendidly bedecked this time, lips painted a glowing yellow-red, cheeks touched with the same color, the rims of her eyes dark with kohl, the eyelids deep green. A muskiness of perfume clung to her. An intricate golden chain lay on her breast; pendant beads of carnelian and amethyst and lapislazuli dangled from it. The presence of her royal lover seemed still to be about her, like an aura. She seemed imperious, magnificent, splendid. For someone her age – she had to be past forty – she was remarkably beautiful, in a chilly, regal way.

And unusual-looking. There was something exotic about her that he hadn't noticed the other time, when he was too dazzled by the whole sweep of Egypt and in any event too sick to focus closely on anything. He realized now that she probably was not an Egyptian. Her skin was much too white, her eyes had an unEgyptian touch of violet in them. Perhaps she was Hittite, or Syrian, or a native of one of the mysterious lands beyond the Mediterranean. Or Helen of Troy's great-great-grandmother.

She seemed strangely tense: a coiled spring. Her eyes gleamed with expressions of – what? Uneasiness? Uncertainty? Powerful curiosity? Even a tinge of sexual attraction, maybe. But she appeared to be holding herself under tight control.

She said, 'The stranger returns, the man from America. You look healthier now. Hard work must agree with you.'

'Yes,' he said. 'I suppose it does.'

'Eyaseyab says you are an ambassador.'

'In a manner of speaking.'

'Ambassadors should present themselves at court, not at the temple of the goddess.'

'I suppose so. But I can't do that.' His eyes met hers. 'I don't have any credentials that would get me access to the court. In all of Thebes you're the only person of any importance that I have access to. I've come to you today to ask for your help. To beg you for it.'

'Help? What kind of help?'

He moistened his lips.

'Two people from my country are living somewhere in Thebes. I've come to Egypt to find them.'

'Two people from America, you say.'

'Yes.'

'Living in Thebes.'

'Yes.'

'Friends of yours?'

'Not exactly. But I need to find them.'

'You need to.'

'Yes.'

She nodded. Her eyes drifted away from his. She seemed to be staring past his left cheekbone.

'Who are these people? Why are they here?'

'Well –'

'And why is finding them so important to you?' she asked.

'It's – a long story.'

'Tell me. I want to know everything.'

He had nothing to lose. But where to begin? He hesitated a moment. Then the words began to flow freely. He poured it all out. My country, he told her, is so far away that you could never comprehend it. There is a Service – a kind of priesthood, think of it as a priesthood – that sends emissaries to distant lands. A little while ago they sent two to a place called Rome, a man and a woman – Rome is very distant, almost as far as my own country – but they went astray in their journey, they traveled much too far, they wandered even as far as the land of the Nile and have not been heard from since –

He listened to himself speaking for what seemed to be half an hour. It must all have been the wildest nonsense to her. He watched her watching him with what might have been irritation or incredulity or even shock on her face, but which was probably just bewilderment. At last he ran down and fell silent. Her face had tightened: it was like a mask now.

But to his amazement the mask suddenly cracked. He saw unexpected tears welling in her eyes, flowing, darkening her cheeks with tracks of liquefied kohl.

She was trembling. Holding her arms crossed over her breasts, pacing the stone floor in agitation.

What had he said, what had he done?

She turned and stared straight at him from the far side of the room. Even at that distance he could see restless movements in her cheeks, her lips, her throat. She was trying to say something but would not allow it to emerge.

At last she got it out: 'What are the names of the two people you're looking for?'

'They won't mean anything to you.'

'Tell me.'

'They're American names. They wouldn't be using them here, if they were here.'

'Tell me their names,' she said.

He shrugged. 'One is called Elaine Sandburg. The other is Roger Lehman.'

There was a long moment of silence. She moistened her lips, a quick tense serpent-flicker of her tongue. Her throat moved wordlessly once again. She paced furiously. Some powerful emotion seemed to be racking her: but what? What? Why would a couple of strange names have such an effect on her? He waited, wondering what was going on.

'I have to be crazy for telling you this,' she said finally, in a low, husky voice he could scarcely identify as hers. He was stunned to realize that she was speaking in English. 'But I can't go on lying to you any longer. You've already found one of the people you're looking for. I'm Elaine Sandburg.'

'*You?*'

'Yes. Yes.'

It was the last thing he had expected to hear. Vortices whirled about him. He felt numb with shock, almost dazed.

'But that isn't possible,' he said inanely. 'She's only thirty-two.' His face flamed. 'And you're at least –'

His voice trailed off in embarrassment.

She said, 'I've been here almost fifteen years.'

She had to be telling the truth. There was no other possibility. She spoke English; she knew Elaine Sandburg's name. Who else could she be if not the woman he had come here to find? But it was a struggle for him to believe it. She had had him completely fooled; she seemed completely a woman of her time. He had memorized photos of Elaine Sandburg from every angle; but he would never have recognized this woman as Sandburg, not in a thousand years, not in a million. Her face had changed:

considerably sharpened by time, lengthened by her journey into middle age. The tight brown curls of the photographs must have been shaved off long ago, replaced by the traditional black Egyptian wig of an upper-class woman. Her eyebrows had been plucked. And then there was the strange jewelry, the transparent robes. Her lips and cheeks painted in this alien way. Everything about her masked her identity: she had transformed herself fully into an Egyptian. But she was the one. No doubt of it, no doubt at all. This priestess, this devotee of Isis, was Elaine Sandburg. Who had given him cuddly Eyaseyab to play with. And had told Eyaseyab to take him across the river to the City of the Dead and lose him over there.

Sudden searing anger went roaring through him.

'You were simply playing with me, that other time. Pretending you had no idea where I was from. Asking me where America was, whether it was farther from here than Syria.'

'Yes. I was playing with you, I suppose. Do you blame me?'

'You knew I was from Home Era. You could have told me who you were.'

'If I had wanted to, yes.'

He was mystified by that. 'Why hide it? You saw right away that I was Service. Why'd you hold back from identifying yourself? And why ship me over to the other side of the river and stash me among the embalmers, for God's sake?'

'I had my reasons.'

'But I came here to help you!'

'Did you?'

CHAPTER SEVEN

Lehman said, 'Where is he now?'

'In one of the temple storerooms. Under guard.'

'I still can't understand why you told him. After chewing me out the way you did last week when I was the one talking about doing it. You made a complete hundred-eighty-degree reversal in a single week. Why? Why?'

Sandburg glowered at him. She was furious – with herself, with Lehman, with the hapless boy that the Service had sent. But mainly she was furious with herself. And yet, even in her fury, she realized that she was beginning to forgive herself.

'Originally we thought he was simply here on an independent research mission, remember? But when he told me that in fact he had come here looking for us – that he had come to *rescue* us –'

'Even so. Especially so. You recall what you said last week? You just want to be left alone to live your life. Your life in Eighteenth Dynasty Egypt. And therefore we can't let him know a thing, you said. But then you did, anyway.'

'It was an impulse that I couldn't overcome,' she said. 'Have you ever had an impulse like that, Roger? Have you?'

'Don't call me Roger. Not here. My name is Senmut-Ptah. And speak Egyptian.'

'Stop being such an asshole, will you?'

'I'm being an Egyptian. That's what we are now: Egyptians.'

They were in his astronomical chamber, a small domed outbuilding behind the oldest shrine of the main Karnak temple. Cool bright sprinklings of starlight penetrated the openings in the roof and sketched patterns on the brick floor. Across the blue-black vault of the ceiling the fantastically attenuated naked figure of the goddess Nut, the deity of the sky, stretched from one side of the room to the other, great spidery arms and legs yards and yards long spanning the starry cosmos, with the Earth-god Shu supporting her arched nude form from below and complacently smiling figures of ram-headed Khnum standing beside him. Dense rows of hieroglyphs filled every adjacent inch of free space, offering intense assertions of arcane cosmological truths.

Sandburg said, 'I was being just as Egyptian as I could be. But there he was solemnly telling me all about the Service, really sweating at it, trying to explain to a priestess of Isis where America was and where Rome was and how two people from this Service of his had overshot their mark and disappeared somewhere in the depths of time – no, wait, he didn't try to tell me it was time-travel, he just used geographical analogies – and suddenly I couldn't hold it in any longer. I couldn't just go on standing there in front of him pretending to be a fucking ancient priestess of Isis, looking lofty and esoteric and mystical, when this kid, this *kid* who had come three and a half thousand years to find us, who I had sent over to the City of the Dead to work as a pickler of mummy-guts because we wanted to get him out of our hair, was begging for my help so that he could find you and me. Our rescuer, and I was treating him like shit. Playing games with his head, making him reel off yard after yard of completely needless explanation. I couldn't keep the pretense up another minute. So I blurted out the truth, just like that.'

'An impulse.'

'An impulse, yes. A simple irrational impulse. You've never had one of those, have you? No – no, of course not. Who am I asking? Roger Lehman, the human computer. Of course you haven't.'

'That isn't true and you damned well know it. You like to think of me as some sort of android, some kind of mechanical man, but in fact I'm every bit as human as you are, and maybe a little more so.' In his agitation he snatched up one of his astronomical instruments, a little gleaming armillary disk from whose center a hippopotamus image yawned, and ran his long tapering fingers around its edges. 'Remember, I was the one who originally wanted to have a little talk with him, to find out, at least, what might be going on down the line. You said you shouldn't do it, and you were right. And then you did it. An impulse. Christ, an *impulse*! Well, I have impulses too, whatever you may think. But even so I still have enough sense not to jump out of a third-floor window simply because I happen to be on the third floor. And enough sense not to say the one thing I shouldn't be saying to the one person I shouldn't be saying it to.'

'If I seriously thought that it could have done any harm –'

'You don't think it can?'

'He's here alone. I've got him in custody. He can't make us do anything we don't want to do. We've got complete control of the situation. Really we do.'

'I suppose,' Lehman said grudgingly. He wandered around the room, fingering his charts and instruments. He rubbed his hands over the bits of gold and lapislazuli embedded in the wall. He picked up three long tight rolls of sacred papyri that he used in his divinations and set them fussily down again in slightly different places. 'How do you think they were able to trace us?' he asked.

'How would I know? Something with their computers, I guess. Calculating probable trajectories. Maybe they took a guess. Or a bunch of guesses. You know they sweat a lot whenever any mission goes astray. So they sweated the computers until they came up with a hypothetical location where we might have landed. And sent this kid to check it out.'

'And what happens now?'

'We go to talk to him. You and me both.'

'Why?'

'Because I think we owe it to him. There's no sense pretending any longer, is there? He's here, and he knows I'm here, and he's probably guessed that you're here too. He's Service, Roger. We can't simply leave him in the dark, now. We've got to make him understand the way this has to be handled.'

'I don't agree. I think the best thing for us is just to keep away from him. I wish you hadn't said anything to him in the first place.'

'It's too late for that. I have. Anyway, he's probably got news from people we knew in Home Era. Carrying messages, even.'

'That's exactly what worries me.'

'Don't you want to hear anything about –'

Lehman gave her a wild-eyed stare. 'Elaine, those people are thirty-five centuries in the future. I want to keep them there.' He sounded almost desperate about it.

'Last week you were hot to hear the gossip,' she said.

'That was last week. I've had a week to think about things. I

don't want to stir all that old stuff up again. Let it stay where it is.
And let us stay where *we* are. I'm not going to go near him.'

His lower lip was quivering. He seemed actually afraid, she
thought. Where had granite-faced Senmut-Ptah gone?

She said, 'We can't simply stonewall him. We *can't*. We owe
him at least the opportunity to talk to us.'

'Why? We don't owe him anything.'

'For Christ's sake, Roger. He's a human being. He came here
with the intention of helping us.'

'I'm aware of that. But –'

'No buts. Come on with me. Right now. You'll be sorry if you
don't. I can guarantee that.'

'You're a terrible woman.'

'Yes. I know that. Listen, do you remember how it was for us
when we first landed here? Helpless, bewildered, hopelessly
lost in time, dressed like a couple of Romans fifteen centuries
out of place, unable to read or write Egyptian, not speaking a
word of the language, not the first inkling of it, hardly knowing
anything about this civilization except what we learned in high
school? Wondering how the hell we were going to survive? You
remember how frightening that was?'

'We survived, though. We did more than survive.'

'Because we were good. We were adaptable, we were
versatile, we were clever. Even so, we went through two years
of hell before we started to make things happen for us. You
remember? I certainly do. Life as a temple whore? You didn't
have to do that, at least, but you had your bad times too, plenty
of them.'

'So? What does that have to do with –'

'This kid is here now, up against some of the same things we
were. And the only two people in the world that he has anything
in common with choose to turn their backs on him. I hate that.'

'What are you, in love with him?'

'I feel sorry for him.'

'We didn't ask him to come here.'

'It was lousy of me just to dump him out on the streets to shift for himself in the City of the Dead. It's going to be lousy of us to tell him that he's wasted his time coming here, that we don't want to be rescued, thank you very much but no deal. How would you feel if you came charging in to be somebody's savior and got told something like that?' She shook her head firmly. 'We have to go to see him.'

'You're suddenly so soft-hearted. You surprise me.'

'Do I?' she said. 'And here I was thinking you were the soft-hearted one. Secretly, behind the grim façade.'

'How discerning you are. But I still don't want to see him.'

'Why not?'

'I just don't.'

She moved closer to him.

'We have to. That's all there is to it.'

'Well –'

'Do you think he's a magician? A hypnotist? He's just a kid, and we've got him locked safely away besides. He can't make you do anything you don't want to do. Come with me.'

'No.'

'Come on, Roger.'

'Well –'

'Come. Now.'

She led him, still grumbling, out of the building, past the temple of Amenhotep II and the pylons of Tuthmosis I and Tuthmosis III, down the avenue of ram-headed sphinxes and into the Precinct of Mut. The storeroom where she had parked Davis for safekeeping was partly below-ground, a cool, clammy-walled crypt not very different from a dungeon. When they entered it, Davis was sitting huddled on the straw-covered floor next to a shattered statue in pink granite of some forgotten king that had been tossed into the room for storage two or three or five hundred years earlier. The Egyptians never threw anything away.

He looked up and glared balefully at her.

'This is Roger Lehman,' she said. 'Roger, I want you to meet Edward Davis.'

'It's about fucking time,' Davis said.

Lehman extended his hand in a tentative, uncertain way. Davis ignored it.

'You look a whole lot older than I expected,' Davis said. 'I would never have recognized you. Especially in that cockeyed costume.'

'Thank you.'

'You expect me to be polite?' Davis asked bitterly. 'Why? What the hell kind of fucking reception did you people give me? You think it was fun, falling across three and a half thousand years? Have you forgotten what that feels like? And then what happens to me when I get here? First she ships me across the river to be an embalmer's apprentice. After which she throws me in this hole in the ground when I come back over. What am I, your enemy? Don't you two stupid monkeys realize that I'm here to goddamn *rescue* you?'

'There's a lot you don't understand,' Sandburg said.

'Damn right there is. I'd like you to tell me –'

'Wait,' Lehman said. Sandburg shot him an irritated look and started to speak, but he held up his hand to silence her. To Davis he said, 'Talk to us about this rescue plan of yours, first. What's the arrangement?'

'I'm on a thirty-day mission. We don't need the full thirty, now that I've found you so fast, but we've got to wait it out anyway,

right? On the thirtieth day they'll drop the jump field into an
alleyway just north of Luxor Temple. It's the one I landed in,
with a graffito on the wall pronouncing a curse on some winemerchant who screwed one of his customers. The field arrives
at noon sharp, but of course we're there waiting for it a couple
of hours before that. The rainbow lights up, the three of us step
inside, away we go. Back home in a flash. You don't know how
hard they've been working, trying to locate you two.'

'They couldn't have been in much of a hurry,' Lehman said.
'Did Elaine tell you we've been here fifteen years?'

'In the Home Era time-line you've only been missing for a
year and a half. And they've been running calculations nonstop
most of that time. I'm sorry we couldn't match up the displacement factors any better, but you've got to understand it
was really just a stab in the dark sending me to the year they did.
We had a twenty-year probability window to deal with.'

'I'm sure they did their best,' Sandburg said. 'And you too. We
appreciate your coming here.'

'Then why did you send me to –'

She held up her hand. 'You don't understand the situation,
Edward.'

'Damned right I don't.'

'There are certain factors that we have to explain. You see,
we don't actually –'

'Wait a second, Elaine,' Lehman said sharply.

'Roger, I –'

'*Wait a second.*'

It was his priest-voice again, his stony Senmut-Ptah voice.
Sandburg peered at him in astonishment. His face was flushed,
his eyes strangely glossy.

He said, 'Before you tell him anything, we need to have a
discussion, Elaine. You and I.'

She looked at him blankly. 'What's to discuss?'

'Come outside and I'll tell you.'

'What the hell is this all about?'

'Outside,' Lehman said. 'I have to insist.'

She gave him a glance of cool appraisal. But he was unreadable.

'Whatever you say, O Senmut-Ptah.'

CHAPTER EIGHT

They stood in the darkness of the garden of the Precinct of Mut. Torches flickered in the distance. Somewhere, far away, the priests of Amon were chanting the evening prayer. From another direction came a more raucous sound: sailors singing down by the riverfront.

Lehman's long, gaunt figure towered above her. Lines of strain were evident in his face. It had taken on the same strange expression that had come over him the week before, the night when she had first told him of the arrival of a member of the Service in Thebes.

'Well?' she said, perhaps a little too harshly.

'Let me think how to put this, Elaine.'

'Put what?'

He made a despairing gesture. 'Wait, will you? Let me think.'

'Think, then.'

She paced in a fretful circle around him. A dim figure appeared on the pylon of a distant temple and unhurriedly began to take in the pennants for the night. Some dark-winged nocturnal bird fluttered by just overhead, stirring faint currents in the warm air.

Lehman said finally, speaking as though every word were very expensive, 'What I need to tell you, Elaine, is that I'm half inclined to go back with him. More than half.'

'You son of a bitch!'

He looked abashed, uncomfortable. 'Now do you see why I told you I didn't want to see him? You yourself pointed out last week that there were risks in talking to him, that it could stir up troublesome old memories. Well, it has.' Lehman touched his hand to his forehead. 'If you only knew how I've been churning inside since he got here. Every day it's gotten a little worse. We should have simply kept clear of him, the way we had always planned to do if anyone came. But no. No. Bad enough that he stumbled right into you first thing. You still had the option of keeping your mouth shut. No, you had to spill everything, didn't you? And now – now –' He scowled at her. 'I was wavering even then, last week.'

'I know you were. I saw it. We talked about it.'

'I was able to put the idea away then. But now –'

'Just seeing him, that was enough to make you want to go back down the line? Why, Roger? Why?'

Lehman was silent again for a time. He scuffed at the ground with his sandaled foot. A young priest appeared from somewhere, staggering under the jeweled and gilded image of a cobra taller than he was, and came stumbling toward Lehman as though wanting to ask him some question about it. Lehman waved the boy away with a curt, furious gesture.

Then in a remote voice he said, 'Because I'm starting to think that maybe we should. We've done all right for ourselves here, sure, but how long can our luck hold out? For one thing, consider the health angle. I don't mean the exotic diseases they have here: I assume our immunizations will continue to hold out. I'm just talking about the normal aging process. We have to keep in mind that this is a primitive country in many ways, especially where it comes to medicine, and we're starting to get older. It won't be easy for us here when the medical problems begin – the big ones, the little ones, the medium ones. You want someone to help you get through your menopause with powdered scarab and a tincture of goose turds and a prayer to Thoth?'

'I'm doing all right so far.'

'And if you develop a lump in one of your breasts?'

'They have surgeons here. It isn't all goose turds and powdered beetles. Why this sudden burst of hypochondria, Roger?'

'I'm just being realistic.'

'Well, so am I. I don't know what you're worrying about. This is a clean, healthy place, if you happen to belong to the privileged classes, and we do. We've kept ourselves in good condition the whole time we've been here and we're in terrific shape right now with no sign of problems ahead and we're going to have really beautiful mummies. What other reasons do you have for going home?'

'I don't know. Homesickness? Curiosity about what's been happening back there? Maybe I've just had enough of Egypt, that's all.'

'I'm sorry to hear that. I haven't.'

'So you want to stay?'

'Of course I do. That hasn't changed. This is where I want to be, Roger. This is the time and place that I prefer. I have a good

life in a tremendously fascinating period of history and I'm
waited on hand and foot and I don't have to put up with any of
the shit of the modern world. I like it here. I thought you did
too.'

'I did,' he said. 'I do. For so many reasons. But –'

'But now you want to go home.'

'Maybe.'

'Then go,' she said disgustedly. 'If that's what you think you
want.'

'Without you?'

'Yes.'

He looked startled. 'Do you mean that, Elaine?'

'If they ask where I am, just don't say anything. Tell them you
simply don't know what happened to me when we overshot
Rome. You came out of the jump field and discovered that you
weren't in Rome at all, that you were stranded on your own in
Thebes, and there you stayed, shifting for yourself, until this
Davis came along and got you.'

'I can't do that. You know what their debriefings are like.
Anyway, *he'd* tell them.'

'Even if I asked him not to?'

'Why would he want to lie for you, Elaine?'

'Maybe he would, if I asked him very nicely. Or maybe he
wouldn't. But in any case, you've just said that you'd tell them
where I am.'

'I'd have to. Whether or not I wanted to.'

'Then I don't want you going back, Roger.' Her tone was cold
and quiet.

'But –'

'I don't. I won't let you do it.'

'Won't *let* me?' he repeated.

'That's right. Not if you'd give me away. And I see now that

that's exactly what you'd do. So I'm not going to let you leave here.'

'How could you stop me?'

She reached out. Her hand rested lightly on his bony wrist. She rubbed her fingertips back and forth over his skin.

Softly she said, 'Maybe I'm putting it too strongly. You know I couldn't stop you if you were really determined to go. But I don't *want* you to go. Please. Please, Roger? What I want is for you to stay here with me. I don't want to be left by myself here.'

'Then come with me.'

'No. No, I won't do that.' She leaned close to him. 'Don't go, Roger.'

He stared at her, mesmerized.

'We can be wonderful together,' she said, smiling up at him. 'We *were*. We can be again. I'll see to that, I promise you. It'll be the way it was for us in the beginning.'

He looked skeptical. 'Will it, now?'

'I promise. But stay. There's nothing for you back there. You're homesick? For what? You want to rejoin the Service? Hop when they tell you to? Let them ship you around to a lot of strange places? The glory of the Time Service! What glory? It's just a job, and a damned hard one. You don't want that anymore, do you, Roger? Or maybe they'd give you a desk job. And a nice little one-room apartment with a view of the Potomac, and in ten years you can have your pension and move to Arizona and sit on your porch and watch the cactus grow until you get old. No, listen to me: You want to stay here. This is the right place for us. You've said it a million times. You have a life here, a damned good one. Your estate, your slaves, your chariot, your observatory, your – all of it. You don't want to go back there and be Roger Lehman again. There's nothing for you

in that. You very much prefer being Senmut-Ptah. Don't you?
Don't you, Roger? Tell me the truth.'

Now he was plainly wavering again, drifting back the other
way.

'Well –'

'I know it's a temptation, wanting to see your own time again.
Don't you think I've felt it too, now and then? But it's not worth
it. Giving up all this.'

'Well –'

'Think about it.'

He looked into the distance. The faint warm breeze brought
the sound of a harp, some temple slave playing to amuse the
elder priests in the Amon Temple.

'Think.'

'Yes.'

She watched him. She saw the knots come and go in his
craggy face. He was adding up the columns in that precise
mathematical way of his, tallying the profits and losses.

'Well?' she said.

'All right,' he told her. He sounded almost relieved. 'Forget
what I've been saying. We stay in Egypt. Both of us.'

'You're sure of that?'

'Yes. Yes.'

'Good,' she said. She grinned at him and winked. 'And now
we ought to go back in there and finish talking to him.'

He nodded. 'Yes. We do.'

'Do we understand each other completely now, Roger?'

'Yes. Yes.'

She gave him a long cool look. 'Let's go back inside, then, and
get it over with.'

'Not there,' Lehman said. 'Not in that miserable musty
storeroom. It's too depressing down in a hole like that. Let's

take him over to my chambers in the observatory, at least. It'll
be a little more civilized, talking to him over there.'

  'If you want to.'

  'I think we should,' Lehman said.

CHAPTER NINE

This part of the Karnak complex that they had brought him to was new to him, a round two-story domed building behind the main temple. Since Roger Lehman's priestly specialty was supposed to be astronomy, the building was surely his observatory, Davis thought. So far as he could recall there had been no trace of any such structure in the modern-day Karnak ruins that he had visited on the orientation trip. Perhaps it had been demolished during the tremendous religious upheavals that were due to hit Egypt after Amenhotep III died.

'How about a little wine?' Lehman asked, with unconvincing geniality. 'This is good stuff, from the royal vineyards in the Delta. The very best.'

'You must have good connections at the court,' Davis said.

'The very best,' said Lehman.

From a cupboard in the wall he drew forth three alabaster drinking-cups embellished elaborately with hieroglyphics and a tall graceful terra-cotta amphora with two small handles and a pointed base. A clay stopper plugged its narrow mouth. As he broke it he said, 'Elaine? Wine?'

'Please.'

Davis took a sip, and then a deeper draught. The wine was sweet and thick, with a raisiny underflavor. Not bad, really. And the cup he was drinking out of was a little masterpiece, museum quality. The room itself, Lehman's private priestly chamber, was splendidly furnished, the walls magnificently covered with dark, vividly realistic murals of gods and demons and stars. It had a look of quiet luxury. Sandburg and Lehman had done all right for themselves in Egypt, especially considering that they had started with absolutely nothing only fifteen years ago, worse off than slaves, having no identities, not even knowing how to speak the language. Lehman seemed to have made himself into an important figure in the scientific establishment, such as it was. And she a high priestess and the mistress of the heir to the throne, no less. Both of them obviously wealthy, powerful, well connected. He had felt sorry for them a year ago when he first had heard the story of their being lost in time, far from the Imperial Rome that had been their intended destination, marooned in some alien hostile place where they were doubt-lessly eking out miserable, difficult lives. He couldn't have been more wrong about that. They had proved to be paragons of adaptability. But of course they were Service personnel, trained to handle themselves satisfactorily under all sorts of unfamiliar and bewildering conditions.

Lehman turned to the cupboard again. This time he took from it a lovely little game-board, ebony inlaid with golden hieroglyphic inscriptions. Thirty gleaming squares of ivory veneer were set into it, arranged in three rows of ten, each square separated from its neighbors by ebony strips. From a box at its base he withdrew a pair of odd curving dice and a handful of pawn-shaped gaming-pieces made of some polished blue stone.

'You know what this is?' he asked.

'A *senet*-board?' Davis said at once.

'They really gave you a good briefing.'

'The works. But I've always been interested in Egypt. I made special studies on my own.'

'You don't know how to play, though, do you?'

'*Senet*? No. The rules are lost.'

'Not here they aren't. Everyone plays it. Soldiers, slaves, construction workers, whores. The king plays it very well. So does the royal astronomer.'

From a corner of the room Sandburg said, 'Roger, why don't you get down to business?'

'Please, Elaine,' Lehman said.

Calmly he arranged the pieces on the game-board.

'It even figures in the Book of the Dead, you know. Spell 17: the dead man plays *senet* with an invisible adversary, and has to win the game in order to continue his passage safely through the Netherworld.'

'I know,' said Davis. 'But I'm not dead, and this isn't the Netherworld. Ms. Sandburg is right. If there's business for us to get down to, let's get down to it.'

'Let me show you the rules of the game first, at least. We arrange the pieces like this. And then – a roll of the dice to determine who the challenger is and who's the defender –'

'Roger,' Sandburg said.

'There. You challenge. I defend. Now, we start at this end of the board –'

'*Roger.*'

Lehman smiled. 'Well then. *Senet* afterward, perhaps.'

He poured more wine into Davis' cup and his own and leaned forward across the table, bringing his face uncomfortably close. Davis saw what fifteen years of the Egyptian sun had done to Lehman's skin: he was as dry as a mummy, his skin drumhead-tight over his bones.

He said, 'About this rescue proposal of yours, Davis. It was very kind of you to take the leap all the way back here for the sake of locating us. And marvelous luck that you found us at all. But I have to tell you: it's no go.'

'What?'

'We're staying here, Elaine and I.'

Staying?

Davis stared. Yes, yes, of course. It all fit together now, their odd fidgety elusiveness; her failure to disclose herself to him the first day, when she had heard him babbling deliriously in English; her sidetracking of him to the City of the Dead; her clapping him in that dungeon-like storeroom once she finally had blurted out the truth about herself. They were renegades. They were deserters. So dumb of him to have failed to see it.

He could hear Charlie Farhad's words echoing in his mind.

The past's a weird place. It can make you pretty weird yourself if you stay in it long enough.

Farhad hadn't been willing to go look for them.

I'm not so sure I want to find out what they've turned into, Farhad had said.

Yes.

'You like it here that much?' Davis asked, after a bit.

'We've settled in,' Elaine Sandburg said from across the room. 'We have our niches here.'

'We're Egyptians now,' said Lehman. 'Very highly placed court figures leading very pleasant lives.'

'So I see. But still, to turn your back forever on your own era, your own world –'

'We've been here a long time,' Lehman said. 'To you we've only been missing a year or so. But we've lived a third of our lives here. Egypt's a real place to us. It's fantastic, it's bizarre, it's full of magic and mumbo-jumbo that doesn't make the slightest bit of sense to modern-day people. But it's beginning to make sense to us.'

'Osiris? Thoth? Gods with the heads of birds and beetles and goats? They make sense to you?'

'In a larger sense. A metaphorical sense. You want more wine, Davis?'

'Yes. I think I do.'

He drank more deeply this time.

'So this place is real to you and Home Era isn't?' he asked.

Lehman smiled. 'I won't deny that Elaine and I feel a certain pull toward Home Era. Certainly I do. I suppose I still have family there, friends, people who remember me, who would be happy to see me again. I have to admit that when you first showed up I felt a powerful temptation to go back there with you when the jump field comes to get you. What is it, a thirty-day mission, you said?'

'Thirty, yes.'

'But the moment of temptation has passed. I worked my way through it. We're not going to go. The decision is final.'

'That's a hell of a thing. Desertion, in fact. Completely against all the rules.'

'It is, isn't it? But it's what we want. We're sorry about the rules. We didn't ask to come here, or expect it or want it. But somehow we did, and we made our own way upward. *Clawed* our way. You think working in a mummy factory is bad? You ought to know some of the things Elaine and I had to do. But we put new lives together for ourselves, against all the odds. Damned fine new lives, as a matter of fact. And now we want to keep them.'

'The Time Service is a damned fine life too.'

'Screw the Time Service,' Lehman said. He wasn't smiling now. 'What did the Service ever do for us except dump us fifteen hundred years from where we were hoping to go?' His long skeletal fingers toyed with the pieces on the *senet*-board. He fondled them a moment; then, in a single swift motion, he swept them brusquely off the board and into their box. 'That's it,' he said. 'That's what we had to tell you. Your kind offer is refused with thanks. No deal. No rescue. That's the whole story. Please don't try to hassle us about it.'

Davis looked at them in disbelief.

'I wouldn't dream of it,' he said. 'Stay here, if that's what your choice is. I can't force you to do anything you aren't willing to do.'

'Thank you.'

Davis helped himself to a little more of Lehman's wine.

They were both watching him in a strange way. There was something more, he realized.

'Well, what happens next?' he asked. 'Now do you take me back to that beautiful little room under Ms. Sandburg's temple so I can get a little sleep? Or am I supposed to catch the night ferry over to the City of the Dead, so that I can learn a little more about how to make mummies before my time in Egypt runs out?'

'Don't you understand?' Sandburg said.

'Understand what?'

'Your time in Egypt isn't going to run out. You're staying here too, for keeps. We can't possibly let you go back. You mean to say you haven't figured that out?'

CHAPTER TEN

At least this time they had given him a room that was above ground-level, instead of returning him to the cheerless subterranean hole they had stashed him in before. He actually had a window of sorts – a rectangular slot, about fifteen feet high up in the wall, which admitted a long shaft of dusty light for five or six hours every day. He could hear the occasional twitterings of birds outside and now and then the distant chanting of priests. And, since the Egyptians evidently hated to leave so much as a square inch of any stone surface uncovered by incredible artistic masterpieces, there were superbly done bas-reliefs of gods on the walls of his cell to give him something to look at: a good old ibis-headed Thoth aloofly accepting an offering of fruit and loaves of bread from some worshipful king, and the crocodile-faced god Sobek on the opposite wall holding a pleasant conversation with winged Isis while Osiris in his mummy-wrappings looked on benignly. Three times a day someone opened a little window in the door and passed a tray of food through to him. It wasn't bad food. They gave him a mug of beer or wine at least once every day. There could be worse places to be imprisoned.

This was the fourteenth day of the thirty. He was still keeping meticulous count.

Through the niche in the wall came the sound of singing voices, high-pitched, eerily meeting in harmonies that made his ears ache:

> *O my Sister, says Isis to Nepthys,*
> *Here is our brother*
> *Let us raise up his head*
> *Let us join his sundered bones*
> *Let us restore his limbs to his body*
> *O Sister, come, let us make an end to all his sorrow.*

He had no idea where he was, because they had brought him here in the middle of the night, but he assumed that he must be in one of the innumerable outbuildings of the Karnak Temple complex. What Sandburg and Lehman intended, he assumed, was to keep him bottled up in here until the thirtieth day had passed and the jump field had come and gone in the alleyway near Luxor Temple. After that they would be safe, since he'd have no way of getting back to Home Era and letting the authorities know where and in what year the two missing renegades were hiding out. So they could afford to let him go free, then: stranded in time just like them, forever cut off from any chance of making his return journey, one more unsolved and probably unsolvable mystery of the Time Service.

Thinking about that made his temples pound and his chest ache. Trapped? Stranded here forever?

Over and over again he tried to understand where he had made his critical mistake. Maybe it had been to reveal the nature of his mission to the supposed priestess Nefret before he knew that she was Sandburg and Sandburg was dangerous. But she had already known the nature of his mission, because he evidently had been muttering in English during that time of delirium. So she was always a step ahead of him, or maybe two or three.

If he had been able to recognize Nefret as being Elaine Sandburg, either the first time when she was taking care of him, or a week later when he had walked back into her grasp, so that he could have been on his guard against –

No, that wouldn't have made any difference either. He hadn't had any reason to expect treachery from her. He had come here to rescue her, after all; why would she greet him with anything other than gratitude?

That was his mistake, he saw. Failing to anticipate that Sandburg and Lehman were deserters who didn't want to be rescued. Why hadn't anyone warned him of that? They had simply sent him off to Thebes and let him blithely walk right into the clutches of two people who had every reason to prevent him from returning to Home Era with news of their whereabouts and whenabouts.

He heard a sound outside the door. Someone scrabbling around out there, fooling with the bolt.

He felt a foolish surge of hope.

'Eyaseyab? Is that you?'

Yesterday, when his evening food-tray had arrived, he had been waiting by the window in the door. 'Tell the slave-girl Eyaseyab I'm here,' he had said through the tiny opening. 'Tell her her friend Edward-Davis needs help.' A desperate grasping at straws, sure. But what else was there? He had to escape from this room. He didn't want to spend the rest of his life in ancient Egypt. Egypt was remarkable, yes, Egypt was astounding, he'd never deny that; but as a member of the Service he had a whole range of human history open to him, and prehistory too, for that matter, and to have that snatched away from him by these two, to be sentenced to a lifetime in the land of the Pharaohs –

The bolt slid back.

'Eyaseyab?'

He imagined her bribing his guards with jewels stolen from Nefret's bedchamber, with amphoras of royal wine, promises of wild nights of love, anything – anything, so long as she was able to let him out of here. And then she and that one-eyed brother of hers, maybe, would help him make his way across the river to the City of the Dead, where he could probably hide out safely in that maze of tiny streets until the thirtieth day. Then he could slip aboard the ferry again, entering Thebes proper, finding his alleyway with the graffito and the palm tree, waiting for the shimmering rainbow of the jump field to appear. And he'd get himself clear of this place. To hell with Sandburg and Lehman: let them stay if that was what they wanted to do. He'd report what had happened – he was under no obligation to cover for them; if anything quite the contrary – and then it was up to the Service. They could send someone else to bring them back. The defection would be expunged; the unauthorized intrusion into the domain of the past would be undone.

If only. If.

Now the door was opening. The dim smoky light of a little oil lamp came sputtering through from the hallway, just enough illumination to allow him to see that the veiled figure of a woman was entering his room.

Not Eyaseyab, no. Too tall, too slender.

It was Sandburg. 'You?' he said, astonished. 'What the hell are you doing –'

'Shh. And don't get any funny ideas. The guards are right outside and they'll be in here in two seconds if they hear anything they don't like.'

She set her lamp down on the floor and came toward him. Close enough to grab, he thought. She didn't seem to be carrying a weapon. He could twist one of her arms up behind her back and put his hand on her throat and tell her that unless she issued an order to have him released and gave him a safe-conduct out of this building he would strangle her.

'Don't,' she said. 'Whatever you're thinking, don't even toy with the idea. You wouldn't stand a chance of finding your way out of here no matter what you did. And you'd be throwing away the only chance you have to salvage things for yourself.'

'Where do I have any chance of salvaging anything?'

'It's all up to you,' she said. 'I've come here to try to help you work things out.'

She came closer to him and pulled aside her veil. In the flickering glow of the lamplight her violet-flecked eyes had an amethyst sheen. Her face looked younger than it did by day. She seemed unexpectedly beautiful. That sudden revelation of beauty jarred him, and he was startled by his own reaction.

He said, 'There's only one way you could help me. I want you to let me out of here.'

'I know you do. I can't do that.'

'Why not?'

'Don't try to sound naive. If we release you, you'll go back to Home Era and tell them exactly where and when we are. And the next time they'll send out a whole crew to get us and bring us back.'

He thought for a moment.

'I could tell them I never located any trace of you,' he said.

'You would do that?'

'If that was the price of my being allowed to go home, yes. Why not? You think I want to be stuck here forever?'

'How could we trust you?' she asked. 'I know: you'd give us your word of honor, right? You'll swear a solemn oath at the high altar of Amon, maybe? Oh, Davis, Davis, how silly do you think we are? You'll simply go back where you came from and let us live out our lives in peace? Sure you will. Five minutes after you're back there you'll be spilling the whole thing out to them.'

'No.'

'You will. Or they'll pry it out of you. Come on, boy: don't try to weasel around like this. You aren't fooling me for a second and you're simply making yourself look sneaky. Listen, Davis, there's no sense either of us pretending anything. You're screwed and that's all there is to it. There's no way we're going to let you go home, regardless of anything you might promise us.'

Her voice was low, steady, unyielding. He felt her words sinking in. He could hear the hundred gates of Thebes closing on him with a great metallic clangor.

'Then why have you come here?' he asked, staring into those troublesome amethyst eyes.

She waited a beat or two.

'I had to. To let you know how much I hate having to do this to you. How sorry I am that it's necessary.'

'I bet you are.'

'No. I want you to believe me. You're a completely innocent victim, and what we're doing is incredibly shitty. I want to make it clear to you that that's how I feel. Roger feels that way too, for that matter.'

'Well,' he said. 'I'm really tremendously sorry that you're forced to suffer such terrible pangs of guilt on my behalf.'

'You don't understand a thing, do you?'

'Probably not.'

'Do you have family back there down the line?'

'A mother. In Indiana.'

'No wife? Children?'

'No. I was engaged, but it fell apart. You feel any better now?'

'And how old are you?'

'Twenty-seven.'

'I figured you to be a little younger than that.'

'I'm very tricky that way,' Davis said.

'So you joined the Service to see the marvels of the past. This your first mission?'

'Yes. And apparently my last, right?'

'It looks that way, doesn't it?'

'It doesn't have to be,' he said. 'You still could let me go and take your chances that I'll cover up for you, or that the Service will have lost interest in you. Or you could opt to go back with me. Why the hell do you want to stay in Egypt so much, anyway?'

'We want to, that's all. We're accustomed to it. We've been here fifteen years. This is our life now.'

'The hell it is.'

'No. You're wrong. We've come up from nowhere and we're part of the inside establishment now. Roger's considered practically a miracle man, the way he's revolutionized Egyptian astronomy. And I've got my temple responsibilities, which I take a lot more seriously than you could ever imagine. It's a fantastically compelling religion.' Her voice changed, taking on an odd quavering intensity. 'I have to tell you – there are moments when I can feel the wings of Isis beating – when I'm the Goddess – the Bride, the Mother, the Healer.' She hesitated a moment, as though she was taken aback by her own sudden rhapsodic tone. When she spoke again it was in a more normal voice. 'Also I have high connections at the court, very powerful friends who make my life extremely rewarding in various material ways.'

'I know about those connections. I saw one of your very powerful friends leaving your temple just as I was arriving. He's crazy, isn't he, your prince? And you sound pretty crazy too, I have to tell you. Jesus! Two lunatics take me prisoner and I have to spend the rest of my life marooned in Eighteenth Dynasty Egypt for their convenience. A hell of a thing. Don't you see what you're doing to me? Don't you *see*?'

'Of course we do,' she said. 'I've already told you so.'

Tears were glistening on her cheeks, suddenly. Making deep tracks in the elaborate makeup. He had seen her weep like that once before.

'You're a good actress, too.'

'No. No.'

She reached for him. He jerked his hand away angrily; but she held him tight, and then she was up against him, and, to his amazement, her lips were seeking his. His whole body stiffened. The alien perfume of her filled his nostrils, overwhelming him with mysterious scents. And then, as her fingertips drew a light trail down the skin of his back, he shivered and trembled, and all resistance went from him. They tumbled down together onto the pile of furs that served him as a bed.

'Osiris –' she crooned. 'You are Osiris –'

She was muttering deep in her throat, Egyptian words, words he hadn't been taught at Service headquarters but whose meaning he could guess. There was something frightening about her intensity, something so grotesque about this stream of erotic babble that he couldn't bear to listen to it, and to shut it off he pressed his mouth over hers. Her tongue came at him like a spear. Her pelvis arched; her legs wrapped themselves around him. He closed his eyes and lost himself in her.

Afterward he sat with his back against the wall, looking at her, stunned.

She grinned at him.

'I've wanted to do that since the day you came here, do you

know that? Ever since I first saw you stretched out on the bed in the House of Life.'

His heart was still thundering. He could scarcely breathe. The air in the room, hot and close and dense, sizzled with her strange aromas.

'And now you have,' he said, when he could speak again. 'All right. Now you have.' A new idea was blossoming in his mind. 'We were pretty good together, weren't we?'

'Yes. I'll say we were.'

'Well, it doesn't have to stop here. We can go back together, you and I. Lehman can do whatever he damned pleases. But we could become a team. The Service would send us anywhere, and –'

'Stop it. Don't talk nonsense.'

'We could. We *could.*'

'I'm almost old enough to be your mother.'

'It didn't seem that way just now.'

'It would in broad daylight. But regardless. I choose to stay in Egypt. And therefore you have to stay too.'

Her words came at him like a volley of punches.

He had almost hoped, for a moment, that he had won her over. But what folly that was! Change her mind with a single roll in the furs? Expect her to walk away from her plush life at Pharaoh's court for the sake of a little heavy breathing? What a child you are, he told himself.

He heard the hundred gates clanging shut again.

'Now you listen to me,' she said. She crouched opposite him, on the far side of the little lamp, under the bas-relief of Sobek and Isis. She was still naked and her body had an oiled gleam in the near darkness. She still looked beautiful to him, too. Although now, in the aftermath of passion, he was able to see more clearly the signs of aging on her. 'You said a little while ago that you think Roger and I are crazy for wanting to stay here. You want to save us from ourselves. Well, you're wrong about that. We're staying here because it's where we want to be. And you'll feel the same way yourself, after you've been here for a little while longer.'

'I don't –'

'*Listen* to me,' she said. 'Here are your options. There's an embassy leaving next month for Assyria. It's an ugly crossing, passing through a pretty desolate stretch of wasteland that someday will be called the Sinai Peninsula. We can arrange to have you become a slave attached to the ambassador's party, with the understanding that at some disagreeable place in the middle of the Sinai you'll be left behind to fend for yourself. That's your first choice. If you opt for it, it's extremely unlikely that you'll ever find your way back to Thebes. In which case you're not going to be here to greet any possible rescuers that the Service may decide to send out to find you.'

'Let me hear some other options.'

'Option Two. You stay in Thebes. I use my influence to have you appointed a captain in the army – it's safe, there's no significant military activity going on these days – or a priest of Amon or anything else that might strike your fancy. We get you a nice villa in a good part of town. You can have Eyaseyab for your personal slave, if you like, and a dozen more pretty much like her. A certain priestess of Isis might pay visits to your villa also, possibly. That would be up to you. You'll have a very pleasant and comfortable existence, with every luxury you can imagine. And when the Service sends a mission out to rescue you – and they will, I'm sure they will – we'll help you deal with the problem of staying out of their clutches. You'll *want* to stay out of their clutches, believe me, because by the time they come for you you'll be an Egyptian just like us. And once you've had a chance to discover what life is like as a member of the privileged classes in the capital city of Eighteenth Dynasty Egypt, you won't want to go back to Home Era any more than we do. Believe me.'

'Are there any further choices?'

'That's it. Go with the ambassador's party to Assyria and end up chewing sand, or stay here and live like a prince. Either way, of course, we keep you secluded in this room for another couple of weeks, until the time of the jump field's return is safely past.' She stood up and began to don her filmy robe. Smiling, she said, 'You don't have to tell me which one you choose right now. Think it over. I wouldn't want you to be too hasty about your decision.'

She kissed him lightly on the lips and went quickly out of the room.

'No – wait – come back!'

He heard the bolt slamming home.

CHAPTER ELEVEN

The days went by, slowly at first, then with bewildering swift-ness, then with an excruciating unwillingness to end. He took care to keep count of them, as he had been trained to do, but he knew there was no hope. Sandburg's last lighthearted words tolled in his brain again and again and again, like the sound of somber leaden bells. He lived in a frozen abyss of despair.

As the time passed he could feel his former existence running out of him as if through a funnel. All his memories were slipping away, every shred of identity: mother, father, school days, girls, books, sports, college, Service, everything. Leaving nothing but an empty shell, gossamer-thin.

He had danced his way through life, *sneaked* his way through, dealt somehow with all the uncertainties and the perils and the cruelties. Held his own. More than held his own. He had done very well for himself, in fact. And then had taken one risk too many; and now the game was up. He had run up against a pair of players who were willing to cast him aside without hesitation and with nothing more than the pretense of remorse.

He had only one day left, now. Tomorrow the jump field would return and wait for him to enter it, and after a little while, whether he had entered it or not, it would take off again for his own era.

I am Nepthys.
How beautiful you are that rise this day!
Like Horus of the Underworld
Rising this day, emerging from the great flood.
You are purified with those four jars
With which the gods have washed themselves.

He stared at the wall. Gradually the weirdly serene faces of the monstrous gods that were carved into it began to emerge out of the darkness. The first light of morning was coming through the slot high overhead. The last day: his final chance. But there was no hope. The door was bolted and would stay that way. The day would come and go and the jump field would leave without him and that would be that.

He stood empty and tottering, waiting for the breeze that would blow him to dust.

But he was surprised to discover that he seemed to be filling again. A new Edward Davis was rushing in. An Egyptian Edward Davis. Already he felt Thebes spinning its web around him, as it had around *them*. A new life, rich and strange. The daily company of Horus and Thoth, Isis and Osiris, Sobek and Khnum. Fine robes; lovely women; fountains and gardens. A life spent playing *senet* and sipping sherbet in his villa and attending elegant parties of the sort portrayed on all the tombs of the nobility across the river in the Valley of the Kings. And eventually to have his own fine tomb over there, where his own splendiferous mummy would be put to rest.

No. No. He was amazed at himself. What kind of insane fantasy was this? How could he even be thinking such stuff? Angrily he thrust it from his mind.

Which left him empty again, marooned, defenseless.

He trembled.

He felt once more the devastating inrush of fear, mingled with savage resentment. They had trapped him. They had stolen his life from him.

But had they really?

Was the situation actually that bad?

> *Horus has cleansed you.*
> *Thoth has glorified you.*
> *The masters of the Great White Crown have abolished the*
>   *troubles of your flesh.*
> *Now you can stand on your own legs, entirely restored.*
> *You will open the way for the gods.*
> *For them you will act as the Opener of the Way.*

They had him. He might as well give in. What choice did he have, really? When they finally let him out of here, he would allow Sandburg and Lehman to help him. And they would, if only out of guilt. He would take full advantage of what had happened to him. Build a new life for himself. He could go a long way here.

He knew the history of the years that lay ahead, after all. The whole thing was there, neatly filed in the electronic memory that the Service had poured into his brain. The upheavals that would come after the death of Amenhotep III and the succession of crazy Prince Amenhotep to the throne, the idealistic religious revolution and the bitter counter-revolution that would follow it, the short and turbulent reigns of Tut-ankh-Amon and the others who would follow him – he knew it all, every twist and turn of events. And could benefit from his special knowledge. He would rise high in the kingdom. Higher than Lehman had, higher than Sandburg. A grand vizier, say. A viceroy. The power behind the throne. The powerful men had lovely titles here. *The Eyes and Ears of the King, the Fan-Bearer at Pharaoh's Right Hand.* Edward C. Davis of Muncie, Indiana, Fan-Bearer at Pharaoh's Right Hand. Why not? Why not? He laughed. It was almost a giggle. You are getting a little hysterical, Mr Fan-Bearer, he told himself.

But then came a bewildering thought. What if he achieved all that – and then a rescue team arrived from Home Era to bring him back? A year from now, say. Five years. They couldn't pinpoint the delivery time all that precisely. They'd know what year they had sent him to, but they couldn't be absolutely certain he'd reached it, and there was likely to be a little overshoot on the part of the rescue mission, too. Five years, say. Ten. Enough for him to get really comfortably established.

The Service will send a mission out to rescue you, Sandburg had said. *They will, I'm sure they will.*

Who? Charlie Farhad? Nick Efthimiou?

Yes. Somebody like that. A couple of the tough, capable operators who always knew how to manage things the right way. That's who he'd have to deal with. But how soon? And was he going to welcome them, when they came?

We'll help you to stay out of their clutches, she had promised. *Because by the time they come for you you'll be an Egyptian just like us.*

He wondered. He didn't know.

Priests were beginning to sound the morning chants at the temple, now. The unearthly music of Amon and Horus and

Anubis came floating through the little slot-like window in the wall. A shaft of bright sunlight poured into his room and lit up the carvings. He stared at the calm figures of the gods: winged Isis, full of love, and mummified Osiris and bird-headed Thoth and smiling crocodile-faced Sobek, high above. They stared back at him.

And then he heard the bolt sliding back. Voices outside: Sandburg's voice, Lehman's.

He couldn't believe it. Here on the last day, they had relented after all! The guilt, the shame, had been too much for them, finally. They were giving him back his life. Tears of gratitude burst from him suddenly. They would want him to cover up for them, of course, when he got back down the line. And he would. He would. Just let me out of here, he thought, and I'll tell any lie you want me to.

'Hello, there,' Sandburg said cheerily. She was wearing some sort of elaborate priestess-rig, white linen done up in curl upon stiff curl and a shimmering diadem in her black ringlets. 'Ready for some fresh air?'

'So you've decided not to keep me here?' he said.

'What?'

'This is the day the jump field is coming back, isn't it? And you're letting me out.'

She blinked and peered at him as though he had spoken in some unknown language.

'What? What?'

'I've been keeping count. This is the day.'

'Oh, no,' she said, with a little laugh. 'The field came yester-day. We found your alleyway, and we were there to see it. Oh, I'm so sorry, Edward. Your count must be off by a day.'

He was bewildered. 'My count – off a day –'

'No doubt of it.'

He couldn't believe it. He had ticked off the dawn of each new day so carefully, updating in his mind. The tally couldn't be off. Couldn't.

But it was. Why else would they be here? He saw Lehman standing behind her, now, looking fidgety and guilty. There were others there also. Eyaseyab, for one. A little party to celebrate his release. In the solitude of his cell he had lost track of the days somehow. He must have.

Sandburg took him by the hand. Numbly he let her lead him out into the hall.

'These are your slaves,' she said. 'I'm giving Eyaseyab to you.'

'Thank you.' What else did you say, when they gave you a slave?

'And a charioteer, and a cook, and some others.'

Davis nodded. 'Thank you very much,' he said stonily.

She leaned close to him. 'Are you ever going to forgive us?' she asked in a soft, earnest tone. 'You know we really had no choice. I wish you had never come looking for us. But once you did, we had to do what we did. If you could only believe how sorry I am, Edward –'

'Yes. Yes. Of course you are.'

He stepped past her, and into the hall, and on beyond, around a row of huge columns and into the open air. It was a hot, dry day, like all the other days. The sun was immense. It took up half the sky. I am an Egyptian now, he thought. I will never see my own era again. Fine. Fine. Whatever will be, will be. He took a deep breath. The air was like fire. It had a burning smell. Somewhere down at the far end of the colonnade, priests in splendid brocaded robes were carrying out some sort of rite, an incomprehensible passing back and forth of alabaster vessels, golden crowns, images of vultures and cobras. One priest wore the hawk-mask, one the crocodile-mask, one the ibis-mask. They no longer looked strange to him. They could have stepped right out of the reliefs on the wall of his cell.

Eyaseyab came up beside him and took his arm. She nestled close.

'You will not miss your old home,' she said. 'I will see to that.'

So she knew the story too.

'You're very kind,' he said.

'Believe me,' Eyaseyab said. 'You will be happy here.'

'Yes,' he said. 'Yes. Perhaps I will.'

The masked priests were casting handfuls of some aromatic oil on a little fire in front of a small shrine. Flames rose from it, green and turquoise and crimson ones. Then one of them turned toward him and held out a tapering white vessel of the oil as if inviting him to throw some on too.

How different from Indiana all this is, Davis thought. And then he smiled. Indiana was 3500 years away. No: farther even than that. There was no Indiana. There never had been. Indiana was something out of a dream that had ended. This was a different dream now.

'It is the Nekhabet fire,' Eyaseyab said. 'He wants you to make an offering. Go on. Do it, Edward-Davis. Do it!'

He looked back toward Sandburg and Lehman. They were nodding and pointing. They wanted him to do it too.

He had no idea what the Nekhabet fire was. But he shrugged and walked toward the shrine, and the priest handed him the vessel of oil. Hesitating only a moment, Davis upended it over the fire, and watched a sudden burst of colors come blazing up at him, for a moment as bright as the colors of the jump-field vortex itself. Then they died away and the fire was as it had been.

'What was that all about?' he asked Sandburg.

'The new citizen asks the protection of Isis,' she said. 'And it is granted. Isis watches over you, now and forever. Come, now. We'll take you to your new home.'